Fri...
Whe...
only... *...pro...*

he turns to Wife, Inc.

* * *

"This Child Is Yours."

A half-dozen emotions passed over Lucas's features. Shock, wonder, pleasure, then fear. "We'll get married right away."

Angela scoffed. "I'm not marrying you because of a baby. I had planned all along to raise my child alone."

"Our child." His eyes narrowed. "That's my child inside you." A little burst of joy skipped through him at his own words, surprising him to the core. "I have rights."

"Oh, no, you don't. And you don't have to be in this child's life."

Anger exploded in his features. "Surely you don't think I wouldn't admit to my own child! Since when have you thought so little of me?"

"Since I knew I was the only one in love in this relationship," Angela said, then ran out the door.

Lucas stared at the empty doorway, then bolted after her. If Angela thought he was going to accept this "I can do this alone" garbage, she was in for a big surprise....

Dear Reader,

Welcome to the world of Silhouette Desire, where you can indulge yourself every month with romances that can only be described as passionate, powerful and provocative!

Silhouette's beloved author Annette Broadrick returns to Desire with a MAN OF THE MONTH who is *Hard To Forget*. Love rings true when former high school sweethearts reunite while both are on separate undercover missions to their hometown. Bestselling writer Cait London offers you *A Loving Man*, when a big-city businessman meets a country girl and learns the true meaning of love.

The Desire theme promotion THE BABY BANK, about sperm-bank client heroines who find love unexpectedly, returns with Amy J. Fetzer's *Having His Child*, part of her WIFE, INC. miniseries. The tantalizing Desire miniseries THE FORTUNES OF TEXAS: THE LOST HEIRS continues with *Baby of Fortune* by Shirley Rogers. In *Undercover Sultan*, the second book of Alexandra Sellers's SONS OF THE DESERT: THE SULTANS trilogy, a handsome prince is forced to go on the run with a sexy mystery woman—who may be the enemy. And Ashley Summers writes of a Texas tycoon who comes home to find a beautiful stranger living in his mansion in *Beauty in His Bedroom*.

This month see inside for details about our exciting new contest "Silhouette Makes You a Star." You'll feel like a star when you delve into all six fantasies created in Desire books this August!

Enjoy!

Joan Marlow Golan

Joan Marlow Golan
Senior Editor, Silhouette Desire

Please address questions and book requests to:
Silhouette Reader Service
U.S.: 3010 Walden Ave., P.O. Box 1325, Buffalo, NY 14269
Canadian: P.O. Box 609, Fort Erie, Ont. L2A 5X3

Having His Child

AMY J. FETZER

Silhouette Desire

Published by Silhouette Books

America's Publisher of Contemporary Romance

To Brenda Rollins

One of the smartest women I know

For the best book signings ever and your loyal customers.
For the welcome you began in RWA Orlando
and never stopped giving. For your encouragement and support.
And for "anointing" a Yankee into the clan of "GRITS."

Thanks

 SILHOUETTE BOOKS

ISBN 0-373-76383-2

HAVING HIS CHILD

Copyright © 2001 by Amy J. Fetzer

Visit Silhouette at www.eHarlequin.com

Printed in U.S.A.

AMY J. FETZER

was born in New England and raised all over the world. She uses her own experiences in creating the characters and settings for her novels. Married more than twenty years to a United States Marine and the mother of two sons, Amy covets the moments when she can curl up with a cup of cappuccino and a good book.

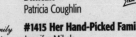
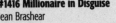

One

"**Y**ou can get pregnant any time, Angela." Her doctor looked up from the test results and smiled across the desk. "You're in perfect health, ready for the procedure."

A little quiver of excitement pulsed through her, then calmed. "I know these donors are screened, but how exactly?" Angela said. She wondered exactly what kind of man donated his sperm for artificial insemination.

"Each donor is tested for disease, abnormal chromosomes, and catalogued by physical characteristics, hereditary traits." Dr. McNair gestured to the booklets, brochures and forms on her lap. "Those will tell you all you need to know."

Yeah, she thought, and how expensive. Each procedure would cost her a tidy sum. And if it took more than two or three, she was looking at some serious debts.

"Are you certain about this, Angela?"

She looked at Joyce, her doctor since she was eighteen, and smiled at the older woman. "Oh, yes." She wanted a baby, a house full of them, and her impatience came from Lord knew where, but it was there. Maybe because she'd turn thirty in a couple of days, and the marriageable men weren't making a beeline to her front door. Or that her sisters were all having kids, and being a doting aunt wasn't enough anymore. Yet it was her job as a late-night radio personality that kept her out of the normal time frame to meet many men. She was asleep when most were awake, and working when people were crawling into bed.

"Well, then, when you make an appointment with the specialist," Dr. McNair said, bringing her out of her thoughts, "I'll fax your records over to Dr. Bashore. She's had very successful results."

"That's what I'm hoping for." Angela stood, said good-bye and left the office. She walked through the hospital clinic and out into the main hall. She moved quickly, guiltily hoping to get out of the hospital before Lucas knew she was here and she was forced to lie. Lie, because she was not going to tell him. At least not until she was pregnant. He wouldn't understand her choices, she knew. Her best friend of fifteen years had a real problem with mothers without fathers. And intentionally getting pregnant without a husband would send him straight through the roof.

Because he'd been the boy without a father and

abandoned by his mother during his adolescence. When she'd met him, he'd been ashamed and embarrassed that his parents didn't love him enough to want him and hid the fact behind a tough exterior that took patience to crack. But it was worth it. *He* was worth it. And although he'd dealt with his feelings and pulled himself up from a lousy beginning to be a great pediatrician, she'd seen Lucas Ryder's old demons come back when it came to single parenthood. Especially because he didn't want children of his own. He'd view her decision as deliberately making life hard on a kid. Like it had been for him.

And he'd try to talk her out of this.

Well, she thought, he could *try*. But she wasn't changing her mind. Not for anyone. Not even for her best pal.

Standing at the nurse's station, Lucas made notes on the chart while his charge nurse, Sandy, waited. "I saw Miss Justice a second ago, Dr. Ryder."

His head jerked up. "Here?" He looked past her to the glass doors leading to the main hall.

"You don't have an appointment for another thirty minutes. You might catch her."

Smiling his thanks, Lucas handed the chart back and checked to see if he had his pager turned on as he headed for the doors. Wondering why Angela hadn't stopped in to say hello, he rushed into the main hall, looking left and right, then catching a glimpse of her near the elevators. He worked his way through the people, most stepping out of his way when they saw the white coat and stethoscope, but his focus was on the redheaded woman. Damn, she looked good in the short green summer dress, the fabric shifting over her figure as she walked. Although he'd known her since he was a teenager and wouldn't dare jeopardize his friendship with her, he was still just a man. And she was one good-looking woman. Lord, if the listeners of KROC radio could see their Love Line doctor now, they'd know that her sexy voice matched her looks.

When he got close, he let out a soft catcall. "Looking hot today, Ange."

Angela tensed for a second, caught, then laughed softly as she glanced back. "Today? Yesterday? How would you know, Ryder?" Discreetly she stuffed the booklet and brochures into her handbag. "I haven't seen you for two weeks."

Lucas swept his arm around her waist and kept walking with her down the hall. "I know, I'm sorry. But you were in the neighborhood, why didn't you stop by?"

She elbowed him. "You know I wouldn't just pop in unannounced. Besides, I really don't have time." Glancing at her watch, she moved away.

"Not even for a cup of coffee?"

He looked so abandoned standing near the staff lounge door. Handsome as hell, but alone. Ha, she thought. Lucas Ryder was never lonely. His dark good looks, blue eyes and the aura of danger that hadn't left him since he was a teenager still lured women like ants to a picnic.

She offered an apologetic smile. "Sorry."

Luc didn't know why he was feeling shoved aside,

especially when he'd canceled on her and most everyone else because of work often enough. But he got the feeling she was avoiding him just now. And that was not like Angela. She shared everything with him.

"Where are you going in such a hurry?"

"I have to go in and do a promo spot for the Water festival, then pick up my dry cleaning and try to catch some sleep before going to work."

He held up his hand. "I get the picture."

"Good, then you understand."

"Yeah, yeah, the life of a celebrity."

"I'm not famous, Luc."

"But too famous to spend some time with your ol' buddy?"

She sighed, shaking her head over his kicked-puppy look. "Come on, buy me some coffee," she said, looping her arm with his and pulling him toward the staff lounge.

His smile widened as he pushed open the door, letting her go ahead and inhaling her perfume as she passed.

Inside, he went to the coffee service, completely oblivious to the young nurses gawking at him, their gazes shifting between her and Lucas, and Angela could read the speculation in their eyes.

It made her smile. What woman wouldn't want to be linked with a handsome man, she thought, taking the cup and settling into the worn leather sofa.

Lucas sat beside her, placing his coffee cup aside, untouched.

Angela sipped, then winced. "That's awful."

He smiled slyly. "I know."

"So you want to send me into intensive care with coffee unfit for the Marines?"

"No, I just missed you and thought the sad lonely boy routine would get to you."

"It was the whining that got me."

"I don't whine."

"See, there you go again."

He laughed, sinking into the sofa and propping his arm on the back. "I have missed you."

Angela felt his gaze travel over her and wondered why it felt intense right now. He'd seen her at her worst, during different stages in their past, but now, it felt as though he were looking at her for the first time. *I'm reading what's not there,* she thought. She loved Lucas, like a brother. A brother.

But looking at him now, with his black hair falling down over his brow and feeling those piercing blue eyes skate over her face, she almost hated that he was her best pal.

The thought made her straighten in her seat.

No. It was the same as it ever was between them. They just hadn't had the chance to get together for the past couple of weeks. That's all it was. That's what it *had* to be.

Smothering her thoughts, she launched into questions about his job. And he was most willing to talk. He loved kids. Loved making them well, loved protecting them. He mentioned his patients by name, told her about the siblings, the parents, and Angela found herself admiring him more that he was one of those doctors that had a really great beside manner and loved not only his work, but the people he treated.

Time got away, and in the middle of the conversation, Angela glanced at her watch, then jumped up. "I have to go."

He stood. "Yeah, me, too." He checked his pager, glad there were no messages. Discarding the paper cups, he followed her out the door. They were near the elevator when she heard someone call his name.

They both looked down the corridor to see a slender, rather busty blonde dressed in red rush up to Lucas. They said hello, and he brushed a kiss to the woman's cheek before introducing them. Angela instantly forgot her name because she couldn't get past the viperous look the blonde shot her. *My word.* It was cool and assessing, staking out her territory on Lucas like a flag on Mount Everest. Angela was tempted to warn her that no woman could rope and tie Luc Ryder, let alone drag him to the altar. The man had a serious case of no-commitment blues. He just liked telling himself otherwise.

"See you later, Luc," Angela said and stepped away.

Immediately, Luc excused himself from the blonde's side and came to Angela. "We still on for dinner next Thursday night? My turn to get the Chinese take-out and videos."

"It's been your turn for the last two times, Luc. You're making up for dumping me to go save some *kid*," she teased, rolling her eyes. He chuckled shortly, and her gaze shifted past him to the latest girlfriend. Angela wondered if this one could handle that she and Luc had been best friends since high school. She had her doubts, but kept them to herself.

"She's lovely Lucas," she said softly. "But I think you'd best quit mentioning me."

He frowned. "I don't." *Not that much*, he thought. Did he?

"Yeah, right." She gave him a playful shove. "The minute you introduced me, she got that 'so this is *her*' look."

"She'll learn." He wondered if any woman would understand their friendship.

"For your sake, I hope so. I've got to go, darlin'."

He caught her arm before she took another step. "What are you doing here, anyway?"

"Annual checkup." That wasn't a complete lie, she thought.

His brows knitted. "Everything okay?"

"Perfect." Ready to be impregnated, she thought, stepping into the elevator and punching the button. Now if she could just find the cash to afford it.

Her gaze on Lucas, Angela watched as the other woman moved closer and touched him freely enough that Angela had no doubt the two had been intimate with each other. It didn't matter that Lucas barely acknowledged his latest conquest. Jealousy speared through Angela like a serpent, startling her. And as the elevator doors closed, she sagged against the wall, wondering when her feelings had taken on such power, and the danger of it to her longtime friendship with Lucas.

A couple of days later, Angela avoided thinking about her risky spurt of jealousy and talked herself into going out on a date to get some distance. She was tightening her earring when the doorbell rang. She flung the door open, expecting her date. Yet she found Lucas in jeans and a T-shirt, holding a paper bag from a local fast-food chain.

So much for emotional distance, she thought, smiling. "Hi, medicine man."

"Hey, yourself. Whoa," Lucas said in a low growl as his gaze swept down her body, from the black silk sheath dress to the dark stockings and high heels. "You look hot enough to fry my eyeballs."

She smiled, putting on the second earring. His compliments had always been good for her ego. "Thanks, but your timing is lousy." She nodded to the bag.

"Hey, no sweat, I just took a chance and lost. So, who's the lucky guy tonight?" He stepped inside and closed the door.

"Randy Costa."

Luc groaned, leaving the bag on the table by the door. "Good Lord, Ange." Randy had a reputation of sweeping women off their feet and right into his bed. "Why him?"

She paused and looked at him. Luc was so clueless sometimes. "Let me see, he's wealthy, handsome as the day is long, has a good job. He's polite. And..." She gave him a dramatic gasp and a surprised look. "Oh, gee! He asked me." Although she had planned on the artificial means of having a family, she wasn't beyond hoping that Mr. Right was out there somewhere and one more date might reveal him. She'd much rather meet him, fall in love and get pregnant the old-fashioned way instead of in a sterile clinic, alone.

Lucas smirked, leaning on the banister. "And you're running late, again."

"It's a consistency thing I'm working for," she said as she rushed up the staircase. Lucas watched her go and glimpsed the lacy tops of her black stockings beneath her short silk dress. The sight shot a hard bolt of desire right through him. The shock of it made him straighten and frown.

Okay, that was new.

Angela Justice was his best friend, his pal. For nearly fifteen years, for the love of Mike. None of his friendships with men, his softball team buddies, his old college roommates or the doctors at the hospital compared to the long-lasting relationship he had with Angela. She was the only person who'd reached out to him when he was a scared and lonely kid dumped in the local orphanage. And she was the only person who continued to be his friend when he'd scared everyone else off. Even the guys.

Oh, he'd always been attracted to Angela. A man would have to be blind not to see how beautiful she was, but he'd never stepped over the line. Never once made a pass at her. Not that he hadn't wanted to when he was young and his testosterone levels were somewhere on Mars. But he was an adult, in control, and he didn't want to ruin the friendship that had taken him through the worst and best times of his life. He tried putting the instance out of his mind, attributing it to a hard day at work.

Yet when she came back downstairs, her hair perfect, a beaded clutch in her hand along with her shawl, his gaze dropped to her legs misted in black.

"You still have the most incredible pair of stems in the county, Ange."

She froze on the last step, a bit shocked by the sultry way he said that. *Don't look for what isn't there,* she reminded herself. "Why, thank you, darlin'," she murmured a little breathlessly, then went to the hall mirror and plucked at her short red hair.

Luc remembered when it had reached past her waist and it drew the attention of half of their high school football team. Of course, those legs in a short cheerleading skirt might have had something to do with it, too, and he wondered when watching a woman primp got to be so darned entertaining. Then his stomach did a quick jump as she bent and ran her hands up her stockinged legs from ankle to thigh in a motion so innocently seductive he wanted to peel those suckers off just as slowly.

Lucas smothered a groan and wondered what had gotten into him tonight.

"So, is this a passable outfit?"

She did a turn in front of him, and Luc felt his blood pressure rise. "Hell, yes." But she didn't look like his buddy anymore, he thought, frowning more to himself than her choice of clothes. "Where are you going?"

"The Theater on the Green."

Wonderful, he thought. In the dark, hidden by trees, Randy would have a good old time with her. "Be careful."

Angela frowned. "This is not my first date with Randy, and if you hadn't been so busy, you would have known that."

"I know, I know. Sorry. At least you can deck him if he gets fresh."

"Fresh?" She laughed softly. "Lighten up, will you? You sound like Daddy."

"Your father wouldn't let you out of the house looking like that," he muttered under his breath, and Luc decided that he needed a distraction, fast, and focused on the half hung curtains and the ladder in the corner of the living room. "Redecorating?"

"Gosh, you're just *so* smart. No wonder you're a doctor."

He made a face at her. "I could have helped you with that."

"I left three messages." She checked the contents of her purse as she added, "You were obviously having a rockin' good time with Denise."

"It was Diane."

She looked up, frowning. "Was?"

"Yeah. It didn't work out."

Her eyes widened. "You were with her just the other day!"

"That's about when it went downhill. I got beeped about two seconds after you left, and she was furious that I didn't have time for her."

"The price of *your* popularity, Doc," she said sympathetically. "And it could have worked out, Luc, but you never let the relationship get past the first couple of weeks."

He stared accusingly at her. "I do, but my schedule puts a lot on hold."

"So what was the real problem, then?" Angela asked as she snapped her handbag shut and left it in a chair with her shawl. She nodded to the kitchen and he followed, his gaze focused on the sexy curve of her bare back in the low-slung dress. Her skin looked warm and soft.

"Luc?"

He mentally shook loose the erotic fantasy that just flew through his mind and took the beer she was offering. "I told you, she couldn't handle my schedule." This was Ange, his buddy. His only family... well, her and her parents, her brothers and sisters and their brood of kids.

"I could believe that if you were still a resident in San Diego, but that excuse is old now, darlin'." Angela cocked her head and studied Lucas. He'd been a tough kid with a chip on his shoulder when she'd first met him. The new boy.

With his imposing height, his dark looks and icy China blue eyes, everyone had been afraid of him. Except her. She'd seen the loneliness in him, the fear of rejection, and the friendship she'd struck up with him had been worth every second. Even when Daddy tried running him off because he thought Lucas was nothing but trouble about to happen. But it didn't happen. The more they said he couldn't do, the harder Lucas worked to prove them wrong. She was proud of him and his success. Although the "dare to get close to me" chip was about gone, his coming to her after every broken relationship was getting old. Even he was treating her like the Dear Abby of the airwaves.

"Know what I think?"

"If I knew what women thought, Ange, I wouldn't be crying in my beer."

She stole a sip, then handed back the bottle. "The day you cry over a woman, Ryder, is the day I can spin straw into gold." She pushed him out of her kitchen, her hands on his shoulders, fingers digging in to his tense muscles. He moaned, almost purring. "I think you're dating women who like your social status and success more than the fact that you heal children."

He slid her a look, then faced her. "You've got more to say, I can tell. Go on."

"I don't think you're looking for deep, so you're not getting deep."

"I'd like to get married some day."

She laughed outright and didn't see his offended look as she walked past and looked out the window for her date. Only Luc's Jaguar was parked in front of the house. She swung around as he made himself at home on her sofa.

"I don't want to be alone forever, you know."

Alone? Never. Single? Oh, yes, she thought. "Okay, if that's true then date women who are marriage material, for heaven's sake. From my perspective, your selection almost guarantees a breakup."

He looked up from peeling the label off the beer bottle, and those blue eyes caught her dead in the heart. God, he was so sexy.

"Luc, honey." She crossed to the sofa and sat beside him. "You're committed to your career far more than anything else."

"Am not."

"Really? You've been back nearly two years and I've seen you twice a month, maybe. And just why did Denise—"

"Diane—"

"Diane dump you?"

"Tired of me canceling or leaving in the middle of a date to get to the hospital." His dark brows drew down. Maybe she had something there. But Diane did mention Angela a couple times when they were dismantling their relationship, and Luc knew she'd been jealous. Was he using his job to protect himself from actually making a commitment like marriage? "She's dating Arty now."

Arthur was the podiatrist at the hospital, she recalled. "See there, one of the marriageable ones would understand, be supportive. And marriage is more than a home-cooked meal and getting your dry cleaning picked up, Luc. Lord, you go through women like diet sodas. It's disgusting."

He resented that. He wasn't that bad. "Look who's talking. What about Andrew?"

"That was two months ago." She made a see-what-I-mean face. "Besides, he thought that because I'm AJ at Midnight, giving advice to lovelorn over the radio, it meant I knew everything there was about sex."

His features sharpened. "Did he try something?"

"Yeah, a lot," she said with feeling. "But I beat him off with an ugly stick."

He grinned. "I'll just bet you did."

The sound of a car pulling into the driveway was accompanied by the flash of headlights through the

windows. Angela stood, grabbing her shawl and
throwing it over her shoulders.

Lucas nearly swallowed his tongue.

"What's the matter? Is it too short? You can't see
the tops of my stockings, can you?"

She walked to the hall mirror and tried to get a
look at her hem. Luc moved behind her, and when
she looked up, she caught his gaze in the reflection.
Her heart instantly skipped to her throat. She'd never
seen him stare at her like that, not since they were
teenagers.

"Lucas...you're looking at me like you want to get
me out of my panties."

His gaze shot to hers, and for a second they just
stared, then he walked closer, giving her a sexy half-
smile. "I've always wanted you out of them, darlin',
except you're too good a woman for a guy like me."

"A pediatrician, financially stable, not too hard on
the eyes? Oh, yeah, you're a real bottom of the barrel
loser."

"You say that now, but I like fried frog legs and I
know how you feel about that."

She shivered with revulsion. "You're right," she
said. "I'd have to kick you out first time you brought
that gunk within smelling distance." She tossed the
edge of the shawl over her shoulder and snatched her
evening bag. "Let's be friends, huh?"

Friends. Why didn't that satisfy him as it usually
had, he wondered as she kissed him quick and sweet.
The urge to pull her close surged through him. He
smashed it down and wondered where his mind had
gone to live, because it sure as hell wasn't in his head
right now.

Two

"**W**hoa, wait a second." In Angela's kitchen, Katherine Davenport set the untouched coffee cup she'd been holding aside. "You are *planning* on having a child alone, with no husband. In the south!"

Angela winced at the censure in her voice. "Kat, this is the twenty-first century, for pity's sake. I have a good job and a nice house and I will be able to work any hours I need to."

"My sorority sister has simply lost her mind." Kat grabbed her arm and led her to the kitchen table. "Sit."

Angela obeyed. "I take it you don't approve."

"It's not my place to do that, but think of the repercussions."

"I have, ever since it ended with Eric last year."

"He wasn't good enough for you."

"Lord, you sound like my father. I loved him, Kat. I loved him more than any man. And I thought we wanted the same things till I thought I was pregnant and told him." Angela sipped her coffee, then set the cup down, the year-old heartache of his betrayal bruising her all over again. "I don't think I've ever been dumped quite that fast. Must have been a record." Eric had been furious, blaming her, accusing her of trapping him, and he was gone before she knew if she was truly pregnant or not. It wasn't like he hadn't participated, and though it turned out to be a scare, the entire incident made her see how selfish he had been. He would have made a lousy father, anyway.

"He *wasn't* good enough for you, and that proved it."

"I know, but my heart didn't listen for a long time."

"Does Lucas know what happened?"

"Yes." Her lips curved a bit. "He wanted to beat the daylights out of him. Instead he beat him at baseball."

"What will Lucas say about artificial insemination?" Retrieving her coffee, Kat slid into the opposite chair.

"Lucas isn't going to know."

Kat's eyes went wide. "Oh, you can't be serious. He's your best friend."

"That's only half of it."

Kat leaned over the table, reaching for Angela's hand and giving it a squeeze. "Talk to me, sugah."

Angela swore she was going to keep this to herself, but the secret felt like a shook bottle of champagne inside her just waiting for its cork to loosen. And she could trust Katherine. "I don't want to tell him, and you must promise he won't learn it from you."

Kat crossed her heart. "Nothing shy of torture would get it out of me."

Angela smiled. "My decision would not go over well with him. *At all.* He was abandoned, forced to live on the streets till the county picked him up and threw him in Anchorage House." The day she'd first seen him came back with the same hard blow to her middle. The epitome of teenage tall, dark and mean as hell, she thought, wearing worn jeans and a tight T-shirt. His shoes were nearly soleless, and he was angry, so angry at the world. "He gets a little nuts when it comes to children. He doesn't want a single one to have to live like he did." Her smile was tender. "I guess that's why he became a doctor. And if he sees one who's been abused—" She shook her head. "He doesn't even want any of his own, Kat. What does that tell you?"

"He's scared he'll do the same thing his parents did." Kat filled it in.

"He wouldn't, I know him. I know him better than he knows himself." She sighed. "But there is no convincing him, either, and that has nothing to do with my decision. Luc has his life and I have mine. And while I don't want him to be angry with me, this is something I want very badly. It's my life, my choice. I've never been that career-minded or I would have used my psychology degree for something more than a love-advice radio show on a country and western station." She paused to sip her coffee. "Don't get me wrong. I love my work, and the celebrity status has its perks, but I would give it all up to fall in love with the right man and have babies." When Katherine simply stared, she added, "Is that so antiquated that I've left you speechless?"

Katherine blinked and swallowed. "I know what you mean," she said hoarsely.

Angela leaned over her coffee cup, meeting Kat's gaze. "I want to be a mom. I want a child. I would rather have a husband who thinks I am the *shiznit* of all women and a marriage license to prove it, but that's not a requirement. I *am* going to have my own family."

"I guess coming from such a great pair like your parents, it's only natural."

She shrugged. "That might have something to do with it. Lord knows I love my brothers and sisters and their kids, but it's not enough. I'm ready to love, Kat. I'm ready."

"Ready for what?"

Both women looked up to find Lucas standing at the kitchen door.

Angela paled. "Ready for a vacation," she lied, smiling and wondering how much he'd heard.

"Well, include me, Ange." He stepped inside, brushing a kiss to Angela's cheek, then winking at Katherine. "Hey, Kat. You look great."

"Thank you, sugah, nice to hear it from such a handsome devil," Katherine said, bringing her empty cup to the sink.

Angela craned her neck to look up at him, recognizing the tension in his features. "Wanna talk about it?"

"Nah. It'd just tick me off." He sniffed the air with great exaggeration. "What's cooking?"

She stood. "Ahh, so that's why you stopped by. Begging for a meal, huh?"

He met her gaze. "I was hoping you'd take pity on me."

"I feel so used."

"You are about the best cook I know."

She went to the stove, then glanced back. "Other than me and my mom, how many women have cooked for you?"

He thought about that. "None, actually."

"Then I guess you're stuck with my Dad's daffodil chili, Ryder." She stirred the chili, turning down the fire.

"I hope you brought some antacids," Kat said.

"I know this doctor who'll give me some." He crossed to the stove, staring into the pot. "Feed me, woman, please."

She elbowed him aside. "Watch it, buster."

She said it with a smile so Lucas knew she wasn't going to deck him. Not that she could. She was just a little thing, he thought, watching her move around the kitchen. He helped her set the table while Katherine put bread in the oven to toast, but the kitchen was too small for three adults to be moving around so much. Angela handed them both a soda and ordered them out onto the back deck.

Standing on the deck outside the kitchen, Lucas

leaned his rear against the rail and looked at Katherine
Davenport. He met her in college and knew her almost as long as he'd known Angela. Though she was
only a couple years older than Angela, their sorority
mother hen, he used to call her, she was every man's
idea of southern grace: beautiful, poised, her long red
hair swept in a twist, her clothes teal-colored and tai-
lored to perfection. There wasn't an inch of her that
wouldn't drive a man crazy with want nor be put off
a little by her austere polish. Luc would bet his salary
that she knew exactly which fork to use at a banquet,
but then, he'd also seen her skin a rabbit faster than
Angela's dad.

A widow now, Katherine owned Wife Incorporated, a company of temporary wives-for-hire out of
Savannah. Her employees were nannies, housekeep-
ers, help for a widower, wedding consultants, even
kid wranglers for busy moms. They were skilled in
all those talents that usually came with a marriage
license. And the business was a huge success. As he
and Kat chatted a bit, a kernel of an idea pushed into
his mind. Yet his attention drifted to Angela again
and again. He stared at her through the glass doors as
she put toasted bread on the table. She looked so cute
in cutoffs and a T-shirt, a far cry from the sexy
woman in black the other night. The reminder sent a
charge of heat through his body, and he knew he
needed to pull back from her until he could control
his feelings. Until he understood what was going on
inside him where she was concerned. Especially when
he'd spent that night thinking about Randy Costa's
hands on her, his mouth on hers and around midnight

recognized he was actually jealous. It was a dangerous emotion for him to deal with when he'd had command of it since he was a kid. Still, he wondered why he was so hot for her now when he'd been around her most of his life. And he knew it went deeper than just sexual attraction, and he tried to understand, was desperate to understand, why his feelings for her had suddenly changed from best friends to even thinking about something more.

His gaze swept over Angela as she filled water glasses. He'd thought long and hard about what she'd said the other night, about him dating women that would guarantee a breakup. He admitted that Diane had been less than supportive and couldn't see that his career meant everything to him. It *was* everything to him. He was sick of getting his heart broken because they didn't understand and decided to step back for a while, see what it was inside him that always chose the wrong woman. To see if maybe Angela had been right.

As if she knew she was on his mind she looked up and smiled. Something hit him hard, dead center in his chest. He smiled back, and knew more than anything that he needed to step back from Angela. He had to quit popping by, bumming meals and griping over his breakups to her.

"Give me one of your business cards, Kat," he said, abruptly looking away. He accepted the embossed card, stuffing it in his shirt pocket as he took a sip of soda. He didn't respond to Kat's quizzical expression. A wife for hire would have all the benefits of a wife—well, except for one—with none of the heartache, none of the feelings of being trapped. And it would separate him from Angela before he did something really stupid and destroyed the only relationship that had kept him sane for the past fifteen years.

It was bad enough that she'd turned thirty with all the hoopla of a Christmas parade, thanks to Lucas and her family. Now life was being downright mean. "Is this a cruel joke, Kat?" Angela said into her cell phone as she stood inside Luc's kitchen.

"You know me better than that, darlin'. He asked for help a few days ago and you wanted something close by."

"Close by, not close to home!"

"There were no other jobs suited to the time frame you needed," Katherine said calmly. "This is perfect. Who else knows him better? You can do this without him ever knowing it's you."

Katherine always was the eternal optimist, she thought. "I know, but—" How was she going to explain that being a wife for hire for Lucas was not what she had in mind? But she needed extra money for the procedures.

"I can get you something else, Angela, but in your area, it might take a while."

Angela sighed, glancing around. "At least he's not a major slob," she muttered into the phone. "And I know where everything is."

"Good, then it will be great pay for little work."

Angela agreed and said goodbye, then put her cell

phone away. She needed the money and didn't care where it came from right now.

She hunted through the lower cabinets for cleaning supplies and his pitifully stocked fridge and freezer for something to cook for supper. Oh, Lord, she thought. No wonder he stopped by her place so often. Poor darling, he didn't even know how to shop for groceries. And at his age! Angela set the frozen meat on the counter, then got to work cleaning his house. She'd been here often enough that it didn't feel strange working here, but tackling the dust bunnies was a job in itself. Later, in the early afternoon, she was dead tired, but satisfied. Chicken and dumplings simmered in a Crock-Pot she'd bet he didn't know he had, since it was still in the box, and she couldn't help but make the house look a little special. This was Lucas's place, after all, and she loved her best friend. He deserved something special.

A few hours later, Lucas stepped into his house and drew a deep breath, inhaling the aroma of something wonderful. Food. Cooked food, he thought with a smile. Leaving his briefcase at the door, he quickly investigated the house, instantly noticing how the wood banister shone, the floors gleamed. The house smelled of lemons and simmering chicken, and he was so eager to taste the supper that he burned his tongue. There was wine chilling, and his "wife" had stocked the fridge with food. He could get used to this, real easy. All the perks and none of the obligations. Or the hassles.

Loosening his tie, he walked into his bedroom, feeling a little invaded when he noticed his laundry neatly folded in the drawers, his shirts pressed and hung in the closet. But it was such a relief not to have to hunt one down, or remember to pick them up from the cleaners, that he didn't care. It was like living in a hotel, his shaving gear neatly laid out and his bed turned down. He was certain this wasn't the norm for a housekeeper, but then what did he know.

Boy, he owed Katherine big-time.

Returning to the kitchen, he served up his dinner, flipped on the TV, kicked off his shoes, then sank into his sofa to eat. He was in bachelor heaven, he thought. But halfway through his dinner, Lucas stopped and looked around the living room. He felt suddenly terribly alone, and on instinct, he reached for the phone. He stilled, drawing his hand back. He wanted to talk to Angela, but she was likely sleeping since she DJ'd on the radio from midnight till five in the morning. Besides, the whole idea behind hiring a wife for hire was to give him some distance before he ruined everything.

But he couldn't stop thinking about her, about how sexy and fresh she looked the other day when Katherine was over and last week when she was dressed to the nines for Randy. He frowned, wondering if she was still seeing Costa, and at the thought of her being with the man, something squeezed down on his chest, leaving him feeling chilled and angry. He set the plate on the table. Get a handle on this, he told himself. He'd known Angela most of his life. Okay, so he'd been away doing his internship and residency in California, but they'd kept in touch, visited each other often during the holidays. Yet for the past two years, since he'd been back home, Lucas knew he'd felt different. The other night, watching her getting ready for her date, was the first time he'd been really aware of the difference. And really aware of Angela as more than his friend. He hadn't seen his buddy then, he'd seen only the woman.

Great. He'd tried to avoid this since high school, always tamping down his libido, satisfied with flirting and honored to just be with her. Her face loomed in his mind, her smile, the lush curve of her mouth, and he wondered what it would feel like to have an all-out hot-and-bothered kiss from her. To feel her body locked around his and taste her skin. Lucas leaned forward, bracing his elbows on his knees and cradling his face in his hands. This was not good. He could not risk his relationship with her. Because Lucas knew if he blew it and made a pass at her, and she turned him down, he would lose more than his closest friend. He would lose the only family he'd ever had.

Then he'd be as alone as he was the day his mother dropped him off at school and never came back.

"Thank you for calling in."

"No, thank *you*," the woman said on the other end of the phone line, then hung up.

Angela smiled, thinking that she at least helped somebody's love life tonight as she leaned toward the microphone.

"You're listening to KROC radio and this is AJ at Midnight, keeping you company till the sun shines on the low country." She turned the dial and the country music went over the air and the light went off on her

console. She sank into her chair, closing her eyes. Just
for a second, she reminded herself. One minute was
all she needed. Lord, she didn't think she'd ever been
this tired and she didn't know how much longer she
could do two jobs and keep up. Late nights on the
radio she could handle. It was rushing to Lucas's
place to make like a temporary wife, so she could be
a mother, that she couldn't. It was almost ironic if she
thought on the matter long enough. But it wasn't the
work, it was the hours. She was awake nearly twenty
hours in a day. But she needed the money. And she
needed some extra sleep.

Her body clock wouldn't let her, it was so twisted.

She'd turned down two dinner dates this week,
knowing she wouldn't make it past the entrée. Falling
in her dinner would make a real good impression, she
thought, not that she was really *that* interested. The
entire time she was with some new man, she silently
compared him to Lucas. It was irritating, and she considered why she found her latest dates lacking. Was
it because she didn't trust her dates and the only man
beyond her father she did trust was Lucas? Or was it
simply that she didn't have to get to know him, and
the whole process of showing your best side, then
finding out the things that drive women crazy later
felt like more of a chore than an exciting pleasure?
Or did it all lie in her heart? The unexpected spin of
unfamiliar thoughts and feelings, each leading to Lucas, made her brows tighten. And her heartbeat race.
A second later a light tap on the glass made her flinch.
She jerked upright and glared at her too-young producer. David stood in his cubicle directly across from

her, frowning, and then switched on the intercom
while country music played over the airwaves.

"Wake up, Angela. You're back in two minutes."

She yawned, nodding.

"What's with you? You look like hell."

"Gee, I can always count on you for compliments,
huh, Dave?"

He blushed. "I meant—"

She waved him off. "I know what you meant. And
I do look in the mirror on occasion, you know." Angela poured more coffee into her mug, sipped, then
leaned back in the chair as the song faded. She spoke
into the mike, her voice soft, her drawl deep and
soothing for the people listening at this hour. They
should all be asleep, for pity's sake.

When her shift was over, she left the studio, drove
very carefully home and decided a shower would
work miracles. She had to get Luc's place done before
he came home. Since she'd been doing it for the past
two weeks, it was clean, and there was little to do but
maintain. An early night, she thought, and she would
leave a message that she wouldn't be working tomorrow. It was Chinese take-out and video night with
Lucas. One of the few times she got to see him. And
she needed some rest.

A couple hours later, she finished her job and was
scribbling a note, attempting to disguise her handwriting, when she heard his car pull into the driveway. She
looked up, and panic seized her when she realized she
was close to being discovered. She swept the first
drafts of the notes into her pocket, gathered her things
and ran to the back door. She heard his key in the lock

just as she was closing the rear door. She didn't take a breath till she was driving on the next road over.

Lucas walked into the kitchen, frowning when he caught the scent of perfume. The fragrance was vaguely familiar, and he called out, but didn't get an answer. This was driving him nuts. Plain crazy, he thought. Curiosity was a deadly thing for a man alone, and his was hammering at him constantly. Who was she? Who was this woman who cooked his favorite meals and knew which wine he liked best? He glanced at the table elegantly set for one. It seemed ridiculous to bother just for him. But this woman did. She left little touches of herself all over the house; hand towels and napkins folded like swans, his mail neatly stacked on his desk, potpourri bowls discreetly hidden yet giving off their cinnamon scent. Even his cereal boxes were stored according to height. That made him smile.

He didn't think anyone in the world did that except him and Angela.

He saw the note and read it, frowning. Ah, fend for yourself tomorrow, he thought. It was just as well. He was having dinner with Angela. Their Chinese take-out and movie night seemed to be the only time he got to see her, talk with her. Yet as he served up the meal his wife for hire had left warming in the Crock-Pot, Lucas wondered if it was wise to be alone with Angela.

In the dark.

On a sofa.

But he couldn't let her know that his friendship and mild attraction for her had developed into something far more dangerous.

Three

"**H**ey," Lucas said, stepping inside Angela's house the next night without knocking.

She smiled instantly, leaving the couch and coming to him. "Hey, stranger." She brushed a kiss to his cheek, taking the bags of Chinese food from him. "You're late."

He followed her into the living room. "I had an emergency at the hospital."

She glanced at him, concerned. "Everything okay?"

"Yeah. I think I worked on the future president of the United States. I swear this little ten-year-old boy was smart as a whip. It was like talking to an adult."

She smiled, dropping onto the couch. That was one thing she loved about Lucas. He adored children. Too bad he didn't want to be a father. She froze, frowning. *Oh, don't even open that door,* she warned herself and laid out the containers.

"He could have diagnosed himself, huh?"

He sat beside her, reaching for the Chinese take-out. Steam poured from the paper containers. "Yes, but setting the broken leg would have been a tough one." Luke filled their plates, pausing to bite into an egg roll. He glanced at her as she helped close the containers, and his gaze fell on the bracelet he'd given her for her birthday. The string of diamonds sparkled against her tanned skin, and he remembered her protests that it was too extravagant. But as far as he was concerned, nothing was good enough for her. And it gave him incredible pleasure to see her wearing it. She hadn't taken it off since he'd put it on her.

"So what's your fancy tonight," she said, interrupting his thoughts. "Shoot 'em ups? Romance? Comedy?" She gestured to the stack of videos on the coffee table.

He examined the titles, then popped one into the VCR. "Be surprised," he said when he wouldn't let her see which one.

"You look too happy, Luc. What's going on?"

"I hired Wife Incorporated."

"Really?" she said, focusing on her plate. "And?"

"It's great. I get all the benefits and none of the hassles."

"Well, see, I told you. Any man who thinks marriage is a hassle doesn't really want to get married."

He looked at her, his gaze moving over her face with concern.

"Speak," she said. "I can see it in your eyes. Something's bugging you."

Plate in hand, he sighed and sat back. "I have to tell you…as a listener, you sounded awful last night. Your voice is hoarse, and you kept stumbling over those advertisement intros."

Her dander went up. She was tired because she was cleaning and cooking for him, and she wanted to tell him to quit making so much work for her!

"Some of us have lousy days, Luc."

"Not you. At least not on the air."

She scoffed. "Yeah, right. Dear Angela, solve my problems on the air for two minutes without knowing the whole story, and then don't worry." It wasn't the first time that she thought she was wasting her psychology degree and should have gone back to a nine-to-five practice.

"Hey, it's just for fun."

"People take it seriously," she said, and hated the sharpness in her voice.

"Yeah, and those same people believe in telephone psychics, too. And as a doctor, I have to say, you look like hell and need rest."

Why did everyone insist on being so danged honest with her this week? "Back off, Luc."

He frowned.

"Don't tell me what to do."

"Ange, I was only trying to point out—"

"That I look like death warmed over. Just what a woman needs to hear." Angrily, she shut off the movie that hadn't even reached the opening credits.

"Hey, hey," he soothed, setting his plate down and shifting toward her. "What's wrong?"

His gentle tone sapped her strength even as it wore her down. "Nothing. I am tired. And yes, I've slept. Now will you just lay off?"

He simply stared.

She groaned. "I'm sorry." She patted his hand, wishing she could tell him how she was feeling, but she didn't even know. She felt confused, and talking things over with Lucas had always helped in the past. But this—well, this wasn't something she could share just yet. And she didn't know when she could. She was deceiving her best friend. She smothered a moan. Now she felt worse, especially when he was looking at her all concerned.

Luc tried not to frown, but she was hiding something. They didn't have many secrets, and he didn't like that she was shutting him out. It stung. But he knew better than to push her. When she was ready, she'd tell him. She always did. Resolutely, he picked up his plate again, toed off his shoes, sank into the sofa and restarted the video. They ate in silence, and as the movie played, the tension eased. They laughed, picked the scenes apart, made snide comments about the cheesy dialogue, then when that was over, they cleaned up their dinner mess before popping in another movie.

Sitting beside Angela on the couch, Lucas was watching Arnold Schwarzenegger demolish another town to get the bad guy when he realized Angela was leaning her head on his shoulder. He looked down and smiled. She was sound asleep, and he shifted her closer, wrapping his arm around her shoulder. She snuggled against him, her body heat seeping into him. He sighed with the simple pleasure of it and kept watching the movie. Yet long after it was over and the room was dark, Lucas held her, wondering why he felt complete peace and contentment. And just how he was going to deal with it.

Her bracelet was missing. The one Lucas had given her. Angela was frantic, tearing apart her house. She'd gone so far as to go back to the studio and search till she remembered having it on when she left the radio station. Now hard fear swept her as she jammed her hand beneath the cushions of the sofa, then tore them off, digging. Nothing. Nothing! Oh, Lord, she should never have accepted it, she thought. This was just like her to lose something so precious to her. Tears burned her eyes, and the worst part was that she'd agreed to go to a Candler Hospital fund-raiser tonight, a yearly duty with her job, yet this time, her escort was Lucas. And he would be here any minute.

She stood and went into the kitchen, looking around. Suddenly she stuffed her hand down the sink drain, feeling, hoping and finding nothing. With a moan of despair, she opened the cabinet under the sink and stared for a second, then went to the closet for her tools. In moments she'd laid a towel down to protect her dress, shut off the water line and was under the sink, opening the elbow joint.

She was struggling with the metal pipe collar when she heard, "Good Lord, Angela. Now I've seen everything."

She flinched, and sorrow engulfed her. Lucas. She thought about pretending nothing was wrong, but in her current state, there was no way around it.

Lucas bent and peered under the sink. "A fine time to do house repairs." *Especially in a red cocktail dress,* he thought, letting his gaze slide over her shapely legs. Fleetingly he wondered if those stockings were the kind with the lace tops like she'd worn for Randy. He shook his head. "Angela, this is silly."

She sniffled, keeping her face averted. "Come back in an hour."

"I can't. We're supposed to be there in thirty minutes. I'm on the board. I need to be there for the presentation."

"Yes," she muttered. "I know." Oh, she didn't want to tell him she'd lost the bracelet already.

Lucas reached for her. "Would you come out from under there, for the love of Mike?"

Sighing heavily, Angela laid the monkey wrench aside and shifted out from under the sink. Lucas grasped both of her hands and pulled her to her feet. Instantly she let go and stepped back. She couldn't look at him and busied herself with smoothing her dress.

"Well, you look ready to go," he said skeptically.

"I am. I just need a minute to freshen up."

His gaze shifted to the mess under the sink. "And you needed to repair the sink before leaving?"

"It's a girl thing, you wouldn't understand." She hurried past him, rushing upstairs for her wrap and evening bag. She took one look at herself in the mirror and she moaned. Her eyes were red. She went into her bathroom to make repairs. The time gave her a chance to get a handle on her emotions. Oh, she was an idiot. What must Lucas be thinking?

She patted on some powder, freshened her lipstick and brushed her hair. She was about to adjust her stockings when she saw Lucas roll around the door frame and lean against the wall.

Very softly, he said, "Are you going to tell me why you were under the sink in an evening dress? Because I couldn't find a damn thing wrong with that drainpipe."

She inhaled. "You didn't run the water, did you?"

"No," he said carefully, frowning.

She let out a relieved breath.

"You were looking for something."

Angela nodded, unable to confess that she'd carelessly lost his gift. Her heart was breaking over it.

"Was it by chance—" He fished in his pocket, then held out his hand. "This?"

The strand of diamonds dangled from his fingertip.

"Oh, thank God," she cried, rushing forward and taking it from him. "I thought it was gone forever." She examined the clasp.

"I fixed it. The clasp was loose," he said, and when she wrapped it over her wrist, he stepped forward to help her secure it. Her hands were shaking.

"It's just a bracelet," he said to her bowed head.

"No, it's not." Her voice broke a bit. "It's priceless to me."

"Why?" he said softly.

"Because you gave it to me."

Something warm ignited in his chest then, spreading through him like wildfire, yet when she continued to stare at her wrist, he tucked a finger under her chin, forcing her head up till she met his gaze. "Aren't you going to ask where I found it?"

Her tapered brows knitted. "Where was it?" she asked, and another wave of panic swept over her.

"In my house, Ange. In fact, it was snagged in my bedspread." He watched the color drain from her beautiful face. "Now. You haven't been to my place in a while. And I know you haven't been in my bed."

His softly spoken words, the mere suggestion lacing through them, sent curls of heat through her body.

"So that can only mean one thing."

"And what might that be?" She swallowed, praying she wasn't caught, then knowing she was.

He took a step closer, gazing down at her. "Why have *you* taken a second job as *my* wife for hire?"

She opened her mouth to respond, but nothing came out.

Then his expression darkened, his blue eyes crystal sharp. "And why the hell did you lie to me about it?"

Her chin jutted out. "I didn't lie. Exactly."

"You just didn't care enough to tell me that you're my wife for hire?"

The accusation in his voice stung. "That's not true, and you know it."

"Yeah." He rubbed his hand across his mouth. "I do. But that doesn't explain why you kept this from me. I should have realized it, though. Who else would know all my favorite foods?" He sighed. "But you should have told me."

"It wasn't any of your business." She moved past him into her bedroom.

He was hot on her heels. "You're my friend. If you needed money, why didn't you come to me?"

"Why should I? I'm capable of earning my own money."

His expression fell.

"I can take care of myself, Luc. And I will get ahead. It'll just take a while." When her child was out of college, maybe, she thought. Oh, she didn't want this discussion to go any further because she knew he would pester and then she'd confess every detail to him like a blathering idiot. She was surprised she hadn't already. But she knew he wasn't going to like her ideas about having a baby without a father. He'd try to convince her not to do it because he grew up without parents, being passed around from foster home to orphanage until he ended up in Anchorage House. Which meant he was one step away from jail, if he hadn't straightened up.

"Let me help, Angel," he said.

She shook her head. Something always melted inside her when he called her that. The endearment made her realize again that she couldn't tell him the truth, not yet, not if she wanted this. And she did want a family of her own and didn't want to be fifty when she realized she'd missed her chance. And there was no law that said she had to have a real live man to do it, right?

"Damn your pride," he growled, and she looked up, meeting his gaze. He was still hurt and angry.

"Luc, darlin'," she said softly. "Would you have

hired me as your housekeeper without Wife Incorporated?''

''Hell, no. I would have given you the money.''

''So not knowing who the mysterious cleaning whiz was was just fine until you found out it was me.''

She had him there. ''Yeah. But—''

''Let me do this myself,'' she interrupted. ''I know you can afford anything, but I can't. And if you fire me, I'll only go work for someone else.''

He sighed and stepped closer, grasping her upper arms. The tendrils of warmth unfurled inside her as she gazed at him. ''Wouldn't dream of it.'' His lips curved. ''I should have seen it coming, you know. No one puts their cereal boxes in order according to height except you and me.''

She laughed shortly, relieved. ''We are a pair, huh?''

His lips quirked. ''Yeah.'' He pressed his lips to her forehead, then pulled her into his arms. He heard her soft sigh, felt her body relax as her arms slid around his waist. Desire gained momentum, and he knew this wasn't wise, but he needed to hold her, to feel her need him.

''We're all right then?''

He ran his hand over her slender spine. ''Sure we are. Or we will be if you promise to get some sleep and not kill yourself cleaning my house.''

''I will. Now are we okay?''

''You bet. We've been through worse, right?'' She leaned back, then stepped out of his arms. Her smile was hesitant, almost forced, and he tried not to frown.

"Now, housekeeper of mine, let's go before we're late." He walked toward the door. "I'll see you downstairs."

She stood rock still as he left, wondering what was going to happen when she finally did get pregnant and he wanted to know who the father was. She didn't want to hurt him, but knew this lie would explode in her face. Maybe, she thought, in the time it would take to earn the money for the artificial insemination procedures, she would find Mr. Right, fall in love and have his babies. Wishful thinking, she thought, yet she held tight to that hope. She checked her appearance, then rushed downstairs.

Luc stood at the base of the stairs, waiting. And Angela's heart did a hard slam in her chest at the sight of him. The man had a definite presence, and despite the black tie and tuxedo, the tough youth who'd wielded a switchblade like most kids jiggled the family car keys still lingered in his eyes. People who knew him weren't aware of the details of his past, but she was. Every single one. *Oh, he's come so far,* she thought, and she loved him all the more for it.

She stopped on the steps, frowning softly.

Like a brother. Yes, she loved him like a brother, she reminded herself, refusing to let the emotions from last week surface. It would ruin everything if she did.

"You okay?" he said softly and she looked at him, felt that ice-blue gaze skip over her, and she wished it could be different. Wished that he wasn't such a great friend and confidant and that he wasn't so against becoming a father himself. *Don't even think about it,* she warned herself. The last thing in the world she would risk was Lucas. Or her heart.

Angela tossed the medical paperwork on the dresser near her bedroom door and shrugged out of her linen jacket. Her first appointment with the specialist was over, at least. She'd filled out the forms, looked through pages of profiles of men who'd donated sperm. She still hadn't made a choice and she still didn't have enough money for the first procedure, but knew that by the time she could successfully track her periods and ovulation, she would. She'd only gone off the pill a couple months ago, and her doctor didn't want any residual effects to slow down the process. The specialist had explained every detail, and turkey baster aside, she was excited. After her appointment, she'd had lunch with Katherine and they'd strolled past the shops on Bay Street, looking at the toys and baby things, even browsing through a maternity boutique. She didn't buy a thing, since she was already strapped for cash with this procedure, but her dreams magnified when she'd held a pair of tiny lace-edged socks in her hand. She could hardly wait.

The phone rang, and Lucas confessed to misplacing his house key and asking to borrow her Wife Incorporated copy. She told him to come over, to let himself in, and after she hung up, she glanced at the time, then rushed into the bathroom. Oh, hell, she thought, her date would be here in less than forty-five minutes. Was this a prediction of the future? Late for everything because she wanted a baby. Thirty minutes later she was pulling on her jeans when a knock rattled the door.

"Come in, Luc," she called, reaching for her shirt.

Lucas froze, his gaze ripping over her bare back as she slipped on the T-shirt and tucked it in. Did she have to be so comfortable about dressing in front of him?

"Want to have dinner with me?"

She faced him. "Bad timing again, darlin'." She sat on the bed to slip on her sandals, then checked her purse for tissues, since the movie was reported to be a real tearjerker. "But I left a chicken casserole in the oven for you at your place."

"Thanks. I'm sure it's great, but—" Lucas noticed how lovely she looked and that she was racing around the house. "You have a date? Again?"

"Again? My, aren't we judgmental, Mr. Different-woman-a-week."

"Touché." Lucas shook his head. That was the old Lucas, he thought. He didn't miss dating all the time. "The key, Ange?"

She turned, pointing to her dresser, then inhaled and rushed across the room just as he looked at the brochures. He reached for his key, his hand stilling midair.

"What the hell is this?"

"Nothing," she said, and tried to take them from him.

His features tightened as he quickly flipped open the colored brochure and scanned the contents. His gaze flew to hers, his eyes glacial. "Artificial insemination? Tell me you aren't thinking about this."

His voice was hard, so like when he was a kid and had that chip on his shoulder.

Angela braced herself for a fight that just might change her relationship with this man forever.

Four

She took the papers and her medical record copies from him and shoved them in her drawer. "I wouldn't have the paperwork if I wasn't."

He paled. "This is why you needed the second job."

She nodded.

"You're really *that* serious about this?"

She held his gaze, hating that this discussion had come so soon and wishing she had more time. Her date would arrive any minute, and she didn't want anyone else to know about this yet. Especially her own family. She still hadn't worked out how she was going to tell them. Her sisters would understand, her mom maybe, but her dad would have a fit, as would her brothers. And then Lucas would have allies.

"How could you want a child without a father?"

Oh, the bitterness in his voice stung worse than the image he painted. "I want a family, Luc, and I don't want to be fifty and changing diapers."

"So you'll subject a kid to life without a father just so you're happy?"

She took offense. "It's not like that. I want to be young enough to enjoy my children while they're young. And I'm not 'subjecting' my baby to anything except my love."

"Well, I spent my life without either parent, and it was no picnic."

"I know it wasn't. I was there for most of it. And this child will have me and my family to love them." She paused and then said, "And you, too."

"Raising a kid under the best of circumstances is tough enough, Ange. I see it every day." When he thought of the kids he couldn't help and the look on the parents' face when he told them their babies would die or be crippled for life, Lucas knew he didn't want to be a parent. Not that he'd seen good parenting close up, anyway, except what he'd experienced in Angela's parents' house.

"I know. And I know how it hurts you sometimes. But you don't want kids of your own, and that's the reason I didn't tell you." He frowned. "I knew you would go ballistic."

"I'm not going ballistic!" he shouted, then looked away, drawing in a deep breath before he met her gaze. "I'm trying to understand."

"You can't." He looked offended. "You're a man. One who doesn't want his own kids. How would you know what it's like to want to hold your own baby instead of nieces and nephews?'' He was cheating himself, she thought. He was a doctor with a loving heart and because of his checkered past, because of the lack of love in his childhood, he couldn't see the hunger inside her and didn't want any part of it.

''But without a husband? Without even a partner?''

''I don't need a husband, and I'll be a great mother when the time comes.''

He heard the crack in her voice and groaned, stepping close. ''I know you will. But why are you rushing the process? You act like your chances have completely vanished. You're still young.''

''I'm thirty, and I'm damned tired of waiting for Mr. Right to come along. Who's to say a guy would make it right, anyway? And I'm sick of giving advice to people on the radio about going after what they want and not doing it myself.'' Angela looked at him, and a fleeting thought skipped through her mind, that the only man she would ever consider a future with would never pledge a forever. She rubbed her forehead, pushing the thought aside. Lucas was her best friend, and having her best friend's baby was not in the cards.

The doorbell rang. ''I don't have time to discuss this. That's my date.'' She grabbed her purse and strode out the bedroom door. He trotted down the stairs after her.

''So what are you doing? Going out to look for daddy donors?''

At the bottom of the staircase, she rounded on him,

her eyes hard as glass. "I ought to knock your teeth in for that, Lucas Ryder."

He deserved that, he knew, but the image wouldn't stay out of his mind and give him peace. And she had been dating a lot lately. "Then just answer the question."

Hurt colored her voice. "I thought you had respect for me." She marched to the door.

He caught her arm before she reached it. "I do, Angel, you know I do. That's why I can't understand why you wouldn't just let this happen naturally."

She scoffed. Men were so clueless sometimes. "I've been doing the natural wait, and frankly I don't see where a man in my life should make the difference of whether or not I have a family." Her hands on her hips, she glared at him, furious. "Do you honestly think I would climb into bed with a man to intentionally get pregnant and then not tell him?" She was shouting. "I'm not sleeping with my dates." She lowered her voice and stared into his blue eyes. "And it's none of your business if I do."

His expression darkened, his eyes narrowing. "You're my best friend. It *is* my business, and I don't know what's worse, a donor you know and don't want to participate beyond a few moments of pleasure in the sack—"

"I ought to slap you for that—"

"—or that you're going to put a stranger's sperm into your body and grow his baby."

"*My* baby," she retorted, glaring. He wasn't listening. He had one track in his mind that had years to form, and he couldn't see beyond it. And she knew he never would.

"We haven't even discussed this man's right to know—"

"No," she cut in, waving a hand in front of his face. "No rights. He signed them away. This is my body, my life and my decision, and I won't discuss it with you."

"You're going to shut me out because I have an opinion?"

"No, but you're satisfied with doctoring kids and not having some of your own. That's *your* choice. Not mine."

"That's because I'm the only person I can count on when it gets tough."

"Gee, thanks a heap, Ryder."

Lucas groaned and felt his heart cave in. He knew she would never do to a child what his parents did to him. "Angela."

Angela smothered her hurt. "Look, if I could have a husband and vows, I'd take them. But it's not happening, so butt out, Lucas." The doorbell rang again. "I have to go."

She flung open the door and found Big John on the other side, smiling.

"Did I come at a bad time?" John said. "Or would you two like to discuss whatever it is out on the front lawn so the whole town gets an earful?"

She looked over her shoulder at Lucas as she adjusted her handbag strap onto her shoulder. "This discussion is over."

"Like hell it is."

She tipped her chin up and gave him a look he
could easily read. He was crossing the line if he said
another word. "Lock up when you leave."

She left with John, pulling the door closed, and
Lucas stood rock still for a moment. It had been a
long time since they'd argued like that, and he was
still reeling from it all.

A baby.

The thought chilled him.

And he didn't know what bothered him most. That
she wanted a baby without a father. Or that she hadn't
planned on including him in any of it.

Lucas couldn't stay home alone with his thoughts.
He'd paced for a half an hour before he headed over
to the Justice house and easily wrangled a dinner in-
vitation from Evan and Sally, Angela's parents. Meg,
Angela's sister, her husband, Jason, and their kids
were there. And one of Angela's brothers and his
family. It was Friday night and almost a ritual to have
this house brimming with noise and people. Lucas
loved it. It was home to him. The only home he'd
ever known.

People littered the back yard, the scent of barbe-
cued ribs still lingering in the air. Torches lit the yard,
staving off the mosquitoes and gnats and showing off
Sally Justice's artful hand in the garden and a mam-
moth wooden swing set.

Tossing the ball, Lucas gave over pitching practice
to Zack's grandfather and walked toward Jason.
"That boy's going to be an all-star," Lucas said to

the boy's father, inclining his head to Angela's nephew.

"Yeah, and let's hope he makes millions and sets his parents up for life," Meg said as she passed, carrying dinner dishes back to the house.

Jason, Meg's husband, laughed and winked at his wife and kept watching her till she had disappeared into the house.

He offered Luc a beer from the cooler, and they popped the tops before sitting on the picnic table and watching the kids play with their grandfather.

"So," Jason said. "Who's the flavor of the week for Doc Ryder, man about town?"

Luc snickered. Jason, Blaine and Ford ribbed him constantly about his women. "None, actually."

Jason's brows shot up.

Lucas explained that he was busy and women didn't understand it or like it. He kept to himself that he'd stopped dating because he was sick of being dumped or dumping them. His career was more important.

"What you need, Luc, is to find something you like as much or more than work."

"Not possible."

Jason sent him an amused look. "That's what I thought."

Meg came out juggling a cake, forks and paper plates. Jason set his beer down and rushed to help her. Taking half the burden, he stole a kiss and whispered something in her ear that made her smile and nudge him playfully.

Luc felt almost jealous. He took his beer with him

as he stepped away and leaned against the low stone wall that surrounded the yard.

He smiled at the activity going on around him. Children played on the swing set. Evan, Angela's father, was giving his grandson pointers on his batting stance. Little Alison, Zack's sister, molded sand in a sandbox. One of Angela's brothers, Blaine, rolled on the ground with his boys as his wife, Sarah, talked with Meg. Sally, Angela's mother, watched it all with the patience of a woman who'd raised six children.

And raised him.

Lucas smiled to himself, remembering a time when Evan had tried to run him off. And he couldn't blame him. He was bad news then, black clothes, spiked hair and that danged tattoo along with his "I'm so cool, I'm freezing" attitude. Her brothers threatened to take him apart if he messed with their little sister, and Lucas mouthing off that he'd do what he'd damn well pleased had started a brawl with all three Justice boys. He'd expected the brothers to squeal, and that would have been the end of his relationships with this family. The fight was still a well-kept secret. And he suspected it had something to do with the fact that Luc had decked all three and left Ford with a cut on his arm. But it wasn't the end of it. Angela had persisted, refusing to give up on him. She'd defied her family, mainly, her father, to be his friend.

She had no real idea of how much she'd saved him that day after school. When he'd seen her coming toward him in her cheerleader uniform, his heart had pounded like a sledgehammer. She'd asked him to walk her home, said some boy was bugging her, but that wasn't the real reason. Pity, maybe, or curiosity. He didn't care. A girl he never imagined existed suddenly did. And she was talking to him. He was older, older than most kids in their sophomore year because he'd run away from the foster parents and orphanages so many times, he'd missed a couple years of school. It was tough, but Angela was there, always finding him in the halls after school, talking to him, and their friendship grew. He'd tried out for the football team for her. Because she'd believed he could do it. He'd made the team and made some friends.

He was still stared at, and guys still picked fights with him just to boast, but Angela was just his pal. He could talk to her about anything, and once when he'd cried about being abandoned, she'd never ridiculed him for it and had simply held him, telling him he wasn't alone anymore and never would be again. He'd wanted to kiss her then, he remembered. Badly. But he hadn't, knowing if he did, he'd ruin their friendship. And he liked being a part of her life. A part of something.

Since then, he'd been privy to the details of her life and she his. Until he'd earned a scholarship and had gone off to college, they'd been inseparable. Even then they'd seen each other often, during holidays and in the summer. One year they'd worked at the same camp as counselors. But when he did his internship and residency their time together grew less and less, yet they grew closer. It amazed him, and he couldn't help recognizing again that she was not sharing with him as she had before.

She wanted a baby, alone. Without a husband, a

father, and Lucas could feel the hackles rise along his spine. It ticked him off. Especially that she hid it from him.

And now she was out with Big John, and, well…hell, his imagination was a nasty thing, and it had sent him here. But he knew Angela. She wasn't stupid and she didn't do things on the spur of the moment. She'd thought this artificial insemination out carefully. Planned it, apparently, around not involving him.

"Uncle Luc! Catch!"

Luc looked up and caught the ball, his hand stinging. An all-star, he thought, tossing it back. His gaze moved over the uncles, aunts, grandparents and cousins. His attention focused on the young couples, the way they seemed to take their joy in their children and not away from each other.

How did they get so lucky?

His mother couldn't manage him, and when she'd dumped him he wasn't exactly in diapers. And his father, hell, Luc wasn't sure the man he remembered was his dad. He hadn't stuck around long enough to make much of an impression, except with the back of his hand.

What made these people so special? Was it simply that they wanted children when Lucas knew his mother hadn't wanted him? He pushed his fingers through his hair, hating the memories tugging at the corners of his mind.

Angela wanted a baby. Bad enough to be artificially inseminated. Despite the fact that it was a common procedure, the thought of her carrying a nameless man's child made him think constantly of the nearly faceless man who was his father. And was never around. He could remember having dreams that his dad would show up and take him away from the orphanages and give him a place he could stay and grow roots.

Angela had given him that by letting him into her family.

But she was keeping him out of any part of the family she was trying to start alone. *She's crazy to do this,* he thought. And he had to make her see the consequences, the drawbacks. Illegitimate children were usually accidents, not intentional. That, he thought, was the bitter truth he couldn't swallow.

Two days later, Angela opened the door, and her smile fell.

Since Lucas had known her, that had never happened and it stung him down to his heels. "You're still mad at me."

"Yes," she said. "And I don't think this is a good time."

"You have company?" He peered past her.

She cocked her hip and slapped her hand on the door frame, blocking the way. "Want to check to see if I've got a man hidden under the bed, just waiting for his testosterone level to shoot up so I can have my way with him?"

He sent her a dry, bitter look. "Very funny."

"It isn't funny. You said some mean things to me the other night."

"I know and I'm apologizing." He glanced over his shoulder at the lighted street. "Aren't you going to invite me in?"

She stared at him for a moment in indecision, and Luc's heart pounded hard and slow as he waited. Man, she was really mad, he realized. Finally she stepped back and waved him on through, and he could breathe again. Not exactly the most welcome greeting, he thought, but he deserved it.

He turned and faced her. "You can't stay mad forever."

"Wanna bet?" She shut the door.

He sighed hard. "Can't we talk about this rationally?"

"You are never rational when it comes to kids and single parenting." She walked past him and into the kitchen.

He followed. "Hey, I know there are people out there who do it all the time, and rather well."

She opened the fridge and offered him a beer. He shook his head and pointed to the soda. "Then why can't you believe that of me?"

"Because...they don't *plan* on being single parents. You are."

She practically slapped the can into his hand. "I know what I'm doing, Luc."

She had that "I don't want to discuss this with you" look. "Ange, honey, look. I'm sorry I went off like a rocket, but try to understand what a shock this was. You kept it from me. You've never done that before. As far as I know."

The hurt in his voice bruised her a bit, but before she'd called a doctor or did her research, she knew where Lucas would stand. On the opposite side of the river. "You know, Lucas, you don't tell me all the details of your life, why should you be butting in mine?''

"You butt into my life all the time, give me advice on my women, my lousy housekeeping."

"This is far more serious than reminding you to pick up after yourself."

He took a step closer, rolling the soda can between his hands to keep from shaking some sense into her. "My point exactly."

Angela gazed at him, into those incredible ice-blue eyes with long sweeping lashes, and wished he'd see things her way. He never would, and she was afraid he'd convince her to not do this. "I just didn't want to fight with you till I had to, and I knew this hit too close to home for you."

"It does, Angel."

Her heart did that little skip when he called her that. Then he stepped closer, brushing her hair off her temple and watching his moves. Finally he brought his gaze back to her.

"Forgive me for saying those things?"

"Yes." She licked her lips, her heart thudding a little. "But you're still thinking that every man I date is a potential donor."

God, she knew him too well. "Yes...I mean, no. I won't think that."

She popped the top of her soda. "Yeah, sure, right," she said, then waltzed past him and into the living room.

Lucas stared after her, then followed like a man on a mission, determined to show her the flaws in her mommy plan.

Five

Angela dropped into the sofa and with the remote turned on the TV. Luc took the control from her and shut it off.

She snapped a hard look at him as he lowered to the sofa beside her. She scooted to the end.

Luc realized that she may have *said* she'd forgiven him, but she really hadn't. "I'm not going to chew your head off, but we need to talk."

"You mean *you* need to talk. I'm done discussing this with you."

"Yes, well, then, that's true. Are you not going to listen to me?"

"No."

"God bless it, Angela!"

She turned her head to look at him, her expression

dry. "You're only going to spout off about single mothers and how I'm being stupid."

"You're the smartest woman I know. Except for this."

She was silent, her cool eyes telling him she was not budging.

"Okay, let's take it from way out, in, say, five years from now. Who is going to show your child how to play ball?"

"Me. I'm better than you, anyway."

"You know what I mean."

"I have enough brothers, and my dad is still fit. And you're here, too, or does this mean you'll walk out of my life?" She held her breath.

"Of course not."

She sighed slowly. "It's a long process, Luc. I've been on the pill for years and have to wait till that's out of my system. Then there is tracking ovulation." She didn't even blush, and it made him realize there was nothing they couldn't talk about. Now. "It hasn't happened yet, Luc."

"But you are determined that it will. You can't just date a little while longer?"

"I am dating! I'd like the conventional way, but where is it written that I have to wait for some man to sweep me off my feet? Some man to wait till he finally realizes he loves me and pop the question? Then be married to him long enough for him to be used to being married and willing to have children?"

"You're not on a time clock."

"Yes, I am. I want to be a mother. You can't understand that because you're a man. So what's the point in discussing this with you?''

"Dammit, Angela! Think about this child. He's going to go to school and everyone will know he doesn't have a father. Being a bastard might not hold that much stigma, but it adds to the troubles teens face every day. I know. I've been there. Kids are not nice when you don't have a dad.''

"You had one.''

"Not around when I needed him. Not to teach me how to stick up for myself when other kids were beating me up in school. And my mother, well, she didn't give a damn.''

"Luc—''

He didn't want her to soothe him like she always did. Not now. "No, just listen to me. I hated every second of growing up without a dad. I didn't know things. Things only a father can tell a son, so I learned on my own, and I have the scars to show it.''

"Honey, I know. But this is me, not you.''

"I'm trying to make you see that if you do this, you're creating another me!''

"That's not true!'' She thrust off the couch, glaring down at him. "And I resent the hell out of you comparing me to a woman who dropped her child off at school and never returned! I will be there. I always will. I was for you, wasn't I?''

"Yes, you were. But you're missing the point.''

"The point is I want my own family and I don't want to be fifty when I start it! And you, who does not want any kids and had a rotten past, can't see that this means a lot to me.'' Her voice cracked, and she turned her back on him, wrapping her arms around her waist.

Regret sank through him, and he plowed his fingers through his hair. "Let's just put it aside for now. We aren't going to agree on it."

"This," she said, "is why I didn't tell you."

"You'd planned to be pregnant before you ever said a thing to me, didn't you?"

She him and met his gaze head-on. "Yes."

His features stretched tight, hurt in his eyes.

Angela felt as if she'd kicked him in the teeth.

He stood abruptly, looking around as if trying to decide whether to stay or go. Finally his gaze landed on her, bleak, injured. "I would have stuck by you no matter what, Angela. But the least you could have been was honest with me."

She felt her emotions cave in on each other. His hurt, his disappointment in her, her needs and determination battled with the fact that she'd just wounded the only man who meant anything to her. Meant everything to her.

Then he headed for the door. She rushed after him, catching his arm. Abruptly he turned and dragged her into his embrace.

"I don't want to lose your friendship over this, Lucas."

It slayed him to hear the tears in her voice. "You won't," he said quickly, closing his eyes, loving the feel of her against him, her arms clinging to him so fiercely. "You won't, I swear."

"You sure?"

He looked down, tipping her chin up, and the urge

to kiss her nearly overwhelmed him. "Yeah, I am."
He brushed the backs of his fingers across her cheek
instead. "We will have to agree to disagree."

Briefly, she closed her eyes, his touch sending tiny
bursts of sensation down to her toes. The power of it
shook her. "All right." Her smile was weak, hesitant.
"You aren't going to fire me as your wife for hire,
are you?"

"Hell, no. I like clean underwear and good food."

She laughed shortly. "You are so easy." She
stepped out of his arms, and Lucas felt suddenly cold
and lost.

"Stay?"

He nodded, and they walked back into the living
room. Lucas immediately went to the half-hung curtains, picking up the screwdriver before he climbed
the ladder.

Angela stood alongside, holding the rod, watching
him, thinking that she was lucky to have him for a
friend and never wanted to hurt him. But now that it
was out in the open, she felt relieved. She'd hated
deceiving him. Yet as he measured and screwed the
bracket into place, her gaze moved over him, his
handsome profile, his broad shoulders, and the same
warm stirring she'd pushed aside since she was a
teenager slithered through her, quick and pulsing. He
looked down at her, reaching for the rod. The instant
she met his gaze, the warmth turned to heat and
ripped down to her toes. She inhaled a sharp breath
and quickly handed over the rod. He frowned for a
second, his gaze narrowing a little before he went to
work. But Angela suddenly ached inside.

He'd looked at her like that last week when she was going out with Randy. Like she wasn't his best friend. As if he'd seen only the woman. Intense, primal. Oh, Lord, this was dangerous ground. It wasn't a matter of when her feelings changed, because she'd always been attracted to him. The question was how was she going to handle this? And were his feelings changing, too? Was the risk, the price of their very precious friendship worth—what? Pursuing it? And if he ran in the other direction, what then?

She'd lose him. Forever.

It would be a change they couldn't take back.

He stepped down off the ladder, studied his handiwork, then looked at her.

He frowned. "You okay?" he said, and she met his gaze, nodding.

Swell, she thought. *Just swell*. Standing before her was the perfect man. And he didn't want the same things she did. He didn't want to be a father. And he was the one man she'd want to father her child. As she had when she was sixteen, she smothered her feelings and smiled at him. "If you're in a fixing mood, I've got a leaky faucet and a loose back porch step that need tending."

He grabbed the hammer and grinned. "Lead the way, darlin'. I'm your man."

No, she thought. *You're not*.

"Take him home, Zack!" Angela shouted. "Out of the park!" She howled and applauded for her nephew as he stood at home plate.

"Good grief, you're a noisy broad."

She smiled and elbowed Lucas, not taking her eyes off Zackary. He swung and hit, the crack of the ball to bat silencing the crowd. "It's outta here!" she shouted, coming to her feet with the rest of the people watching the Little League game. Her nephew bolted like a madman, obviously not taking any chances although the ball sailed high and over the fence. The opposing team groaned, and Zack's home run brought two runners in.

Angela did the happy dance, whistling like a sailor on a two-day leave.

Luc knew she had the urge to run down there and hug the little eight-year-old but wouldn't, afraid she'd embarrass him. So she hugged everyone around her, including him. Lucas held her a little longer, but she didn't seem to notice. It was the closest he'd been to her in days, their fight cutting a line between them that made him hurt inside.

They hadn't discussed her mommy plan since that night last week, and she'd sworn him to secrecy. He wouldn't breathe a word, but was still hoping to talk her out of it. It wasn't that he didn't want her to have what she wanted, far from it, it was that he knew this was not the way to go about it.

And he didn't want a child, especially Angela's, to grow up without a father and suffer like he had.

Someone called her name, and Angela scanned the crowd, her gaze falling on Big John, another DJ from the station. Lucas felt himself tense as she excused herself and maneuvered her way down the bleachers toward the man. She'd gone out with him twice since the night Lucas had discovered Angela's secret plan to artificially inseminate. Tall and the size of a bear, John towered over her, but the instant she was near, he swept her into his arms and brushed a kiss to her mouth.

Lucas tamped down the urge to punch the guy and looked away, studying the crowd. But his gaze kept straying to her. All afternoon men had flirted with her, and he knew it wasn't just because she was the most popular radio personality in two states. She was bright, pretty, had a figure that men lusted to touch, but every time he saw her with a man, Lucas saw a potential donor for her baby plan.

It made him grind his back teeth till they ached.

When the next inning began, Angela returned to her seat beside him.

"He ask you out again?"

She looked at him, frowning. "Yes, he did. Why do you ask?"

"Well, his eyes never left your breasts the whole time he was talking to you. I was wondering if he wanted to date them."

She reddened, and it occurred to her that he was right. But then it also told her Lucas was watching her very closely to notice. "They go where I go," she said, forcing a smile.

"And that one." He nodded to the tall, slender blond man standing near the batting cage. "He ask you out, too?"

"That's Jack O'Flynn's father, and yes, we're all going to the movies tomorrow night."

"Well, then, you could have a ready-made family with him," he said. "He's got two kids already."

Angela's eyes narrowed. "I'm not on some obsessed craze to be anyone's mother, Lucas. And dammit, it's not your business who I date."

He looked offended. "I'm just watching out for you, that's all."

"Oh, really," she said bitterly. "Is that what you were doing when you dragged me away from talking with Seth Martin yesterday at the team barbecue?"

"He's not good enough for you, Angela. For crying out loud, he's been divorced twice!" And looking at Angela like he wanted to make her wife number three, he thought.

Her gaze hardened. "A failed marriage doesn't make anyone a loser. Look at me, I've made a ton of mistakes."

"Yeah, well, you would have married Eric."

Her expression fell, her hurt clear. "No, Lucas. That situation just pushed him into revealing his true colors. I would never have married that man, *any* man, because of a baby. That isn't required. And I would *never* marry a man who didn't want kids."

He sipped his soft drink, schooling his features so she couldn't see how her words affected him. Especially since he didn't understand why her words felt like a door slamming in his face. "Guess that puts me out of the running, huh?"

She laughed uneasily, although her heart took a sharp drop to her stomach. "I need your friendship more," she said softly, leaning against him, her head on his shoulder. He looked to the side, smiling when she batted her lashes dramatically. He nudged her, and they laughed and continued watching the game.

Angela focused her gaze on Zackary, not daring to look at Lucas. Because it just now hit her that he was sounding as if he was jealous. And, instantly, she paled. If he was jealous that meant his feelings *had* changed, and that scared her. After all these years could she take this relationship over the line? No, she thought, he didn't want the same things as she did. She wanted a family, he didn't. It was that simple and that defining. They could never have more than what they had now. Because to ruin that with intimacy would only hurt them both and do irrevocable damage to their friendship. He was just being overprotective because he knew her plans to be a mother, she reminded herself. He was watching out for her, telling her the truth. These men weren't the prime picks. But Angela wasn't looking for perfection.

She was just hoping for love.

Angela pushed open Lucas's back door, juggling his dry cleaning, two bags of groceries and her purse while trying to make it to the kitchen counter before she dropped everything. She managed, blowing a wisp of hair out of her face, then headed to his bedroom with the dry cleaning. She frowned as she passed the bathroom, then stopped cold when she entered the bedroom.

''That little stinker,'' she whispered. The room was spotless.

She hung up his cleaning and left the bedroom, searching through the rest of the house. There wasn't a thing out of place. Not even a bit of laundry to do.

Did he think this was helping? Paying her for doing nothing!

She went into the kitchen and put away the groceries before starting supper, slamming pots and cabinets as her temper rose. She thought seriously about scorching his dinner, but her mama taught her not to waste food. She covered the pots and turned them off, knowing he wouldn't be home for another hour.

When she returned the following day, she found the same meal still on the stove, the house still spotless. Panic jumped through her, and she reached for the phone, dialing his practice. In a few minutes she learned that Lucas had been at the hospital for two days. She tossed out the uneaten meal, and a half-hour later she was on the pediatrics floor, moving through the clinic to the ward beyond.

She smiled at Sandy and stopped at the desk. "May I go in?"

"I don't think that would be a problem." Sandy leaned closer, her voice low. "Maybe you can get him out of there and convince him to eat something, at least."

"I plan to," Angela said, then quietly pushed into the room. Three beds were empty, but the one by the window held a little girl with gold blond hair. Lucas was slumped in the chair beside the bed, asleep.

Angela's heart spun with pride, and she wondered if anyone really knew how dedicated he was. This wasn't the first time he'd pulled on all-nighter with a young patient. And he was known for personally calling patients' parents with test results, hounding labs to not make the families wait. She remembered once when a patient hadn't come in for a follow-up, he'd driven to the boy's home and discovered that the father had had to work and the mother was without a car or money to get the boy to the hospital. Lucas had taken the child and his mother in himself, then driven them home, with a stop at a fast food-chain on the way home. He was caring and sensitive to the children of this town. He spoke at schools on career day and spent two days a month at the retirement homes, checking blood pressure and just listening to complaints. His actions, his constant dedication made her admire him more and understand that his career was his world. His only true commitment.

Taking a couple steps, she reached the foot of the bed and looked at the little girl, her heart breaking at the sight. She couldn't be more than five or six, her breathing even but shallow. There were a half dozen tubes running in and out of her, yet the heart monitor wasn't hooked up. That was a positive sign, she thought, but really didn't know enough to judge.

Gently, she touched Lucas. He roused slowly, blinking, rubbing his palm across his forehead as he straightened. He stood immediately, hovering over the child, flipping out his penlight and checking her eyes, then her pulse. He sighed dispiritedly and listened to her heart for a second or two, then turned.

He stopped short when he saw her. Then he smiled. "Ange."

It sounded as if he'd just been tossed a lifeline on a sinking ship. "Hey, medicine man. You look beat."

He ran his fingers through his already mussed hair. "I'm okay."

Her gaze moved over his clothes. "And like you've slept in those."

"I didn't really have time to go home."

"Can I talk you into a taking a break for a little bit?"

His brows rose with surprise, then his expression saddened. He looked at the child. "I don't know…"

"I'll sit with her, Dr. Ryder." A voice came from the doorway as one of the second-year student nurses stepped inside.

He nodded. "I'll be just down the hall. Buzz me if there's any change."

The young woman nodded and took a seat beside the bed. She lifted a storybook from the stack on the side table and began reading. They left the room, but before he could do much else, Angela maneuvered him into the doctor's lounge.

He barely noticed.

Angela pushed him into the sofa, then sat, focusing on the cooler and duffel bag she'd left on the coffee table before going into the ward.

Lucas watched her unload piles of food, unwrapping sandwiches, apples and milk. "So what brought on this burst of charity?"

"Well…my temper, actually." She flashed him a quick smile. "I was shoot-fire angry because I'd thought you were patronizing me by cleaning up your house." He opened his mouth to speak but she put up a hand to stop him, pressing a sandwich into his hand. "This morning I realized you hadn't been home to mess it up."

From the duffel bag she brought out chips and a

thermos of fresh coffee Lucas knew was way better than the stuff sitting on the burner all day. "So if I wasn't here—" he pointed to the floor with the sandwich "—you would have bashed me with a frying pan next time I saw you. Do I have that right?"

"Yup, would have cold-cocked you a good one."

He smiled tiredly. "I wouldn't patronize you, Ange." He bit into the sandwich, the first taste making him hungrier for more.

"Took me a bit to realize that." She poured him a cup of coffee, handing it over before she fished in the bag again. "I brought your shaving gear, and in there—" she pointed to the locker with his name stenciled on it "—is a fresh change of clothes." She set the shave kit on the table.

Lucas gazed at her, deeply touched that she'd worried about him enough to come by and check. More so that she knew exactly what he needed right now. None of the women he'd been with had done anything like this, and if he didn't know how special she was to him before, he did now.

He reached out, closing his hand over hers. "You didn't have to do this."

"I know." She squeezed his fingers. "But you needed backup and you would never ask for it."

He brought her hand to his lips, giving it a soft kiss. "Thanks, Ange."

Angela stared at his mouth on her hand, entranced by the sight. Her heart did a quick tumble in her chest, and she realized she wanted him to keep going, trailing his mouth up her arm…to her lips. Her breathing increased. Her skin warmed. *Don't think about it,* she told herself.

"You're welcome," she managed to say, then pulled free to pour herself a cup of coffee. Wrapping the cup in her hands, she blew on the hot liquid when she really wanted to reach over and brush his hair off his brow, massage his shoulders because he looked so strained and tired. "You should take a shower. It won't do her parents any good to see you like this."

She was right, of course. Slowly, he told her about the little blond girl. That she'd slipped on a trampoline and hit her head. She had a severe concussion and she hadn't woken in two days. Lucas was scared she never would.

"She will. She has the best doctor watching over her," she said, laying her hand on his upper arm.

He smiled weakly. "I've done everything I could and called in the neurologist, but it's just wait and see. God, I hate telling parents that." Every time he did he felt as if he wasn't doing enough.

"But it's all you can do, Lucas. You've exhausted your options."

He swallowed the last bite and dusted his fingertips, then reached for the carton of milk, draining it without stopping. Then he picked up his shaving gear, took his clothes from the locker and headed to the bathroom. He paused, looking back. "Can you hang around a bit?" She was his only bright spot today.

She glanced at her watch. "Sure, I have time before I go on the air."

He nodded and slipped into the bathroom. A few minutes later he came out wearing dark slacks and a button-down shirt with a fresh lab coat. And he was smiling. He was taking a last sip of coffee when Sandy popped her head in.

Lucas tensed and set the cup down. Angela stood slowly.

Sandy smiled. ''She's awake, talking, and her parents are here.''

Lucas grinned, and as the nurse disappeared he instinctively reached for Angela out of sheer want and pulled her roughly into his arms.

''Oh, Luc, I'm so happy for you and for her.''

He knew she meant it. He closed his eyes, knowing that every victory in his life, even the small ones, had meant more because she was here to share them with him.

Six

Lucas was late for the game, having spent the last hour counseling an intern over his lack of bedside manner with his young patients. Pushing the thought out of his mind, he tossed his jacket into the back seat of his car, then loosened his tie as he hurried toward the ball field. The KROC radio station was playing a softball game against the Savannah Sand Gnats for charity. KROC was losing by three runs, yet no one seemed to care.

Climbing up next to Angela's sister, he smiled at Meg, then searched the field for Angela at her position at first base. He grinned. Dressed in a green uniform, her cap pulled low, she was bent over, shifting from side to side, punching her fist into her mitt and hollering at the batter. She looked great, except for the golf-ball-size wad of gum in her mouth making her cheeks bulge.

He hadn't seen her in nearly a week, yet he'd thought about her constantly, about how she'd come to him when he needed someone, how she was the only one who had noticed he wasn't around. And how much he'd wanted more from her. He suspected she was avoiding him, considering every time they got on the subject of her mommy plan they fought.

The batter made a strike, and Angela called him a name, teasing him. He winked at her, then pointed the bat toward the outfield, and Lucas heard Angela shout, "In your dreams, buddy," before the player swung. The crack silenced the crowd as the ball went high but not far. Angela watched it sail, her attention on catching the pop fly and not on the runner.

Nor was the runner watching where he was going.

Lucas rose slowly as the minor-league player plowed right into Angela, bringing her off her feet and sending her flying backward. She hit the ground hard.

And she didn't move.

Oh, God.

Lucas was off the bleachers and hurdling over the fence in seconds. Players crowded around her, calling her name. The hitter was on his knees beside her, apologizing and taking the glove off her hand.

"Don't touch her!" Luc yelled, pushing his way through the people. "I'm a doctor." He knelt beside her. "Angela?" He took her pulse, then checked her mouth for that wad of gum. Relieved that it wasn't lodged in her throat, he realized she wasn't getting any air. Her solar plexus was tight and contracted. Panic shot through him as he bent over her, quickly checking her neck for breaks. He spread her arms, tipped her head back and started CPR. The instant he pressed on her chest, her eyes flashed open as she gasped for breath over and over, yet couldn't get any air into her lungs. Lucas slid his hand under her back and lifted her slightly as she sucked in a huge gulp, then tried to capture more air.

Relief overwhelmed him, choking his heartbeat. She'd just had the wind knocked out of her, but still she hadn't moved much.

"Stay still," he told her when she tried sitting up. "Just try to breathe slowly, in short breaths, till your solar plexus expands."

Angela coughed and rolled to her side, moaning.

"Don't move!"

"I'm all right, Doc. See?" She sat up straight, coughing and still trying to breathe.

"Where does it hurt?"

"Nowhere, Lucas." Pain laced the back of her head, and she rubbed it. "I'm all right."

"The hell you are," he growled, and scooped her in his arms and stood.

"Lucas," she said, frowning at his concern and chalking it up to a doctor thing. "Put me down."

"Forget it." He strode across the field toward the first aid booth.

"You're being overly cautious." The crowd cheered, and Angela waved over his shoulder at them, smiling as her head throbbed.

"I'm a doctor, it's my job to be alert, dammit."

At that, her brows drew down, and she noticed his features, more than concern making them harsh. And his heart was pounding so hard she could feel it thrum into her skin. And she knew he wasn't winded.

She looped her arm around his neck and swore his heart sped faster.

What was up? He wouldn't look at her, his lips pulled tight, his pace nearly a run. He'd seen her injured before. She was notorious for being the only person to leave a ball field limping when everyone else came away unscathed.

Then he turned his head and met her gaze.

Angela was struck dead in the chest at the look in his eyes. Concern and fear, sure, but there was something else, a glitter she'd never seen before. And it fairly shouted at her. Demanded she see it. But she just wasn't sure and longed to know exactly what lay hidden behind his ice-blue eyes. She'd always been able to read Lucas. Better than anyone. Better than himself. But lately, she felt as if she were walking in fog when she was around him. His attitude toward her was changing, and for the first time in fifteen years, she didn't know what to expect next.

Lucas held her tightly, relishing the feel of her in his arms while trying to get a handle on his fear. He was a physician, used to emergencies, yet the picture of her hitting the ground and not moving kept flashing through his mind like a tape on rewind, torturing him. He'd felt helpless for those few seconds. God, if she'd broken her neck, if she'd died playing a stupid ball game, he knew he'd never survive.

Angela was a part of him. A big part. If he lost her... He couldn't even think about it without feeling as if emptiness was strangling him.

He ducked into the first aid tent and laid her on the cot, kneeling beside her. The emergency medical technician on duty handed over his equipment as Lucas examined her.

"I'm going to allow this, Lucas, because you don't want to take my word for it that I'm all right."

"Good. Because I'm doing it anyway." With a penlight, he studied her eyes, frowning as the tech removed her cleats. He sent the EMT out for ice packs for the bruise on the back of her head.

"Gee, this is the first time we've played doctor."

His gaze flashed to hers. She was smiling. He wasn't.

"Hey, lighten up."

"You could have broken your neck."

"Yes, maybe, but I could have done that walking down the stairs, so don't go doing the 'you shouldn't be playing ball' routine on me."

"And if you're pregnant?" he said in a low voice.

She inhaled. Coming from him, the words sounded so intimate, so sexy, conjuring images of getting that way with him. She swallowed and pushed the picture out of her mind. Making love to her best friend was out of the question because she wanted more and he didn't. Ever. "Not that it's your business, but I haven't had the procedure yet, Lucas." Was that relief she saw in his eyes?

"You know you can't be doing this kind of stuff once you are."

"I hadn't planned on playing ball while I was pregnant."

"You're still determined to go through with it, though, aren't you?"

She shoved him back when he went to examine her eyes again. "Good grief, Luc, are you looking for an excuse to infuriate me?"

"Of course not. I'm trying to be realistic, because apparently you can't be." They were silent as the tech came in and handed over the ice pack, then left. Lucas pressed it to the back of her head, and she winced.

"I don't want to discuss this now." She sat up, holding the ice pack as she swung her legs over the side of the cot.

"Okay, fine. But you have to come to the hospital with me."

"No way." Not when he was acting like this, she thought, then stood. Instantly she swayed, dropping the pack and reaching for him. He caught her, and she braced her hands on his upper arms and tried to clear her vision.

"You might have a slight concussion, Ange. We need to get an X ray."

"A concussion? You're overreacting."

He shook his head slowly.

And she remembered the little blond girl who'd walked into the hospital, climbed into bed and hadn't woken for days. Angela rubbed the back of her head. It wasn't bleeding, nor was there much of a lump rising, but she'd have a hell of a headache by tonight.

"Let me be sure, okay?"

The concern in his eyes touched her soul, and she

agreed. At least he wasn't hounding her with his opinion on artificial insemination anymore. She had just enough money saved for the first procedure, and she wasn't going to change her plans. Not when that was all she had. "Fine. Let's go."

After she put on her cleats, they left the ballpark and headed to the hospital. Lucas didn't leave her side, scowling darkly, pacing while they waited for the X rays to be developed, then bringing her into the room as the radiologist read the films. She didn't have a concussion, but Lucas suggested she stay overnight. The radiologist agreed.

"Forget it. I'm not wasting bed space for this."

"Angela. You have jostled your brain," he gritted through clenched teeth, advancing on her till she was up against the exam table. Her heart leaped into her throat as his body pressed into hers and she saw heat flicker in his eyes before his expression closed and he took a step back.

She fought the urge to grope for him, bring him harder against her, and said, "Come on, Lucas, this is silly." It was her day off from the radio station and her Wife Incorporated job, and she wasn't going to spend it in a hospital bed, bored to tears.

"Will it be silly if you fall asleep and never wake up?"

Good grief, he was such a downer today.

"Do you trust my judgment as a physician?" he asked softly.

The question seemed to lay their trust on the line, and she pressed her palm to his cheek, gazing into his blue eyes. "Of course I do, darlin'. You're the best."

Her touch sent tremors of heat through to his bones, and before Luc did something stupid, he grasped her hand and gave her knuckles a quick kiss. "Then check in for the night."

"It's a waste of nurses and doctors when they could be attending to people who really need help. How about I go home and promise to rest and watch movies, be a slug?"

He thought about that for a second. "Agreed, but not alone. I'm staying the night."

At the thought of him sleeping in her house, her skin flushed beneath her baseball uniform. "Baby-sitting? Now who doesn't trust who?"

"I know you, Angela, you won't behave. You never do."

She had to smile at that, then nodded, pushing away from the exam table. "I'm going to warn you, though. I'll be a princess, a real diva. Make you wait on me hand and foot. You know, paint my toenails, peel me grapes." He grinned. "That'll teach you to try to be the boss of me."

Chuckling to himself as they walked to the door, Lucas knew he'd have to sit on her to keep her from doing everything herself. "I get to choose the movies then."

"Deal."

They left the hospital, Lucas's arm tucked around her waist when she swayed a bit. Her cleats made a click click on the tile floor, the metered tap counting off like a ticking clock. For Angela, it seemed to chant his name with the beat of her heart, and she leaned into his warmth, wanting so much more and not daring to take it.

For Lucas it reminded him that he'd have hours alone with Angela and just how hard it would be not to tell her what his heart was saying to him every minute of the day.

Later that night, Lucas watched her sleep, wondering what she was dreaming about because she was smiling. A little tinge of jealousy raced through him. Was she dreaming of a man? Or the baby she wanted so badly? He'd seen the pregnancy and childbirth books all over the house earlier. The sight of them kicked reality right in his face. She was going to do it no matter what he said. And he almost felt jealous of a child that didn't exist. The baby would take her away from him. And he wondered how much of Angela he would lose because he didn't want kids of his own.

His gut twisted, and he rubbed his fingers across his mouth, wishing he understood his own feelings. But all he experienced was complete confusion. When he was apart from her, he could at least concentrate and put his emotions in neat little compartments, past, present, no future that he could see. For his career he had to be a little detached, though inside he wasn't. But with Angela, lately all it took was one look, one smile or innocent touch, and it was like he was a teenager, an outcast, and the most beautiful girl he'd ever seen wanted to be his friend.

He was a mess.

And he had to do something about it. But even broaching the subject, telling her he was falling for her in a way that had nothing to do with being pals, was a risk in itself. All he knew in his heart was that he loved Angela Justice and somewhere during the last couple of years, since he'd come back to the only place he'd called home, that love had taken a sharp and dangerous turn.

He left the chair and sat carefully on the bed, his gaze moving over her flawless face and landing on her mouth, curved in a sleepy smile. He reached, brushing a red lock of hair from her cheek, and he realized his hand was trembling.

He swallowed, his chest tight and burning, the hopelessness of his situation beating him with his own want of a woman he could not have, should not touch.

She wanted babies. He couldn't be a father. Anyone's father. He'd be lousy at it. And he was terrified.

Terrified that he would lose her to this baby plan.

Terrified that he would be alone and without this woman in his life.

And scared as hell that if he didn't do something, he would go stark raving mad.

The timer on his watch went off, making him flinch, and he switched it off, then bent over and cupped his face in his hands.

Oh, God. What am I doing?

He scraped his hands over his face as he looked up and glanced at her. When she was asleep, he was at least without options, but awake, Angela devastated his senses.

"Angela, wake up."

She curled toward him, blindly taking his hand and pulling it to her chest.

Lucas froze, sensations scattering through him like fire. The feel of her warm skin against his was enough to send him over the edge, to take her in his arms. For a moment he didn't move, his body and heart wanting to touch her so badly, to taste her skin, feel her mouth beneath his like he'd dreamed about for the past weeks.

Damn.

Damn, damn, *damn.*

He couldn't keep thinking like this! But he was. Oh, Lord, he was.

"Angela, wake up," he said briskly, pulling free.

"Go away," she muttered and curled deeper into the bedding.

"You have to wake up." He shook her again, praying that sheet didn't slip further down. And silently wishing it would.

"Get lost, Ryder!"

"You need to wake up."

"Gee, you think because I'm talking to you that I just might be awake?"

"Good Lord, you're cranky."

"You get roused every two hours and see what it's like."

He wasn't going to mention that he hadn't slept much, either. "I like you better asleep."

"Good, 'cause that's where I'm going." She still hadn't opened her eyes.

"I don't know why I bother when you're such a mean cuss."

She opened one eye and swung it toward the alarm clock. "It's four in the morning!"

"You're usually on the air right now, so be a brave little patient and sit up. Now."

With a groan of compliance she did, rubbing her face.

The sheet dropped, exposing the swell of her breasts in the skimpy chemise, and Lucas looked his fill, aching to push the thin strap down and put his mouth on her flawless skin. He swallowed and glanced at his lap as she took a sip from the juice glass on the bedside table.

"Happy?" She set the glass down and glared at him.

"Yes." Leaning forward, he checked her eyes, pleased that her pupils had remained the same throughout the day and night.

Angela clenched her fingers in the bedsheet, fighting the urge to move just a fraction and bring her mouth to his. He smelled wonderful, woodsy and so very male, and she knew she had to get away from him to collect herself. When he leaned back, declaring her fit, she tried to get out of bed. He was in the way.

She glared, almost hating the feelings rushing through her.

He smiled. "Brat," he said, then scooted back.

She slipped from the bed, almost running to the bathroom. Lucas watched her go, his body growing tighter with every step she took. The skimpy chemise shifted around her body like air, brushing her thighs, her sweet behind, showing off the lush fullness of her breasts and driving images of stripping it off her

through his tired mind like a battering ram, daring
him to explore.

Angela closed the door and sighed against it. Every
time he woke her she grew more and more agitated.
Not from lack of sleep—she was used to strange
hours with her job—but because when she woke he
was there, smelling great, looking sexy and handsome, and then every time she fell into a dream, Lucas was there. Touching her, peeling off her clothes
and pushing his body into hers.

Tingles of pleasure swept over her skin, tightening
her nipples and sending a quick wash of desire down
to her thighs and curling between. It was just too easy
to imagine them together, making wild jungle love.
And she wanted him. It was a fact she'd been trying
to ignore. She wanted him enough to nearly pull him
into her bed just then. With a moan of frustration, she
pushed away from the door. Using her mouthwash
and splashing water on her face did little to banish
the images floating through her mind and through her
dreams.

What would he think if he knew she'd dreamed of
him? That she had been having less than platonic
thoughts about him?

He'd run.

Despite that she knew his feelings had changed.
Despite that when he looked at her, it was different
and deep and lusty. The two of them didn't want the
same lifestyle, and she had to remember that.

And she had to talk to him about this. She couldn't
go on. Turning sharply, she flung open the door. He
was gone. Crossing the room, she grabbed her robe,

then slipped it on as she trotted down the stairs. She found him in her living room.

Barefoot, he paced before her unused fireplace like a caged animal.

"Lucas."

He stilled, then his head shot up, his gaze flashing her with a look so hot her knees went weak.

"What's wrong?" She crossed the room slowly, feeling as if she'd explode any second. He was razor still, the muscles of his chest straining against his dark T-shirt, his thumbs hooked in the belt loops of his jeans, his hips cocked. He looked at her through a shock of black hair, and Angela thought she'd be swallowed by the desire in his eyes.

It's real, chanted through her head. *He wants me. Oh, God.*

"Lucas, talk to me."

"I have to leave." Yet he didn't move.

A sinking feeling washed through her. "Okay, let me get your medical bag." She started to turn away.

"No, Ange, I meant permanently."

She spun around, her eyes wide. "What! For good?"

He nodded.

"No!"

"God, Ange," he groaned. "I don't want to leave."

"Then don't! I can't believe you're saying this. My God, you just came home!" Just the thought of him gone was like a living thing eating at her soul. Tears welled in her eyes. "Tell me why?"

He didn't answer. But she knew.

She rushed forward, gripping his upper arms as if he would bolt out of her life right now. "Lucas, no, no. This is because of my plans for motherhood, isn't it? You're so opposed you can't bear to look at me." He didn't respond. Her gaze searched his, her heart pounding as she realized he held himself stiffly, his arms at his sides. His features were sharp, harsh. "I'm sorry you feel this way." Her voice broke as she let go and took a step back.

Lucas reached for her and in one motion dragged her into his embrace.

Angela froze, her throat working repeatedly as her body meshed to his, soft yielding to hard. She'd never been this close to him, and she felt every solid inch of him against her, hard and strong and sexy.

Heat and impatience rode between them like a racehorse at full speed. His breathing escalated, his gaze raking her features. Then he plowed his fingers roughly into her hair and tipped her head back.

"You know it's not the reason, Angel," he growled. "And I've waited too damn long to show you why."

His mouth crashed down on to hers.

And fifteen years of suppressed emotion erupted in a storm of longing and passion neither could stop.

Seven

The explosion was tremendous. Powerful. Greedy with impatience.

Their kiss was devouring, a hot slide of lips and tongues and the demand for more. Much more.

Lucas groaned at her wild response, the feel of her touching him like a lover for the first time. He wanted her so badly he couldn't think, could scarcely breathe, yet he moved on instinct. As if through his life he'd known it would be like this. As natural as breathing and as demanding as his need for air.

Sensations poured through him, sapping his strength. His will.

And when she made little eager sounds, nearly climbing onto him, begging for more, he gave it, taking her mouth harder, deeper.

She drove her fingers into his hair, plundering wildly, pausing only long enough to drag air into her lungs and mutter, ''What took you so damn long?'' then kiss him again.

Lucas wanted to roar with sweet victory, his hands diving inside her robe and up the contours of her spine. He filled his palms with her breasts.

Angela cried out against his mouth, his touch emptying her mind to the sensations running through her and fighting for supremacy. This was Lucas, her Lucas! Yet it felt completely right to be kissing him, as if this were the only place she should be. Could be. With the only man she wanted. And now that the opportunity was here, she couldn't get enough of him.

His thumbs circled her nipples, deeply, with a determination to drag every moan out of her, every purr and gasp. And it was working, the sensations familiar, yet each bearing a new and vibrant power, ripping through her blood. Because it was him.

Her hands were everywhere, exploring the width of his chest, the span of his back, his hips. Then she realized he was trembling.

And so was she.

The fresh excitement of it drove her on, and she tore at the hem of his shirt, peeling it off over his head and giving in to the fantasy of her life. She tasted his skin with hot frenzied motions, nipping, laving, and he groaned harshly as she dragged her tongue down over his throat, his chest, then circled his nipple.

He clutched her, his passion gaining speed with hers, and he pushed his hand beneath the silk nightie, stroking her flesh, seeking her delicate center, and Angela's fingers dug into his shoulders.

"Lucas, oh, Lucas." The anticipation was going to kill her!

He found her, wet and hot, and the knowledge undid him. He parted her, his gaze locked with hers as he thrust two fingers inside. Angela flinched and arched, pushing his touch deeper. Rocking. Her body pulsing with mindless greed for him, inside her, filling her. Now. Without hesitation she opened his jeans and sent the zipper down, then slipped her hand inside.

Lucas slammed his eyes shut and quaked with hard shudders.

She stroked him. He played with her. Eyes locked, breath staggering. They didn't waste another moment as excitement slashed through them. Her robe hit the floor. Seconds later, the sliver of a nightgown followed. Then his mouth was on her breast, lips drawing on her nipple before he lowered to his knees, cupping her buttocks and hurriedly bringing her softness beneath his mouth. Angela moaned, her breath no more than a weakened pant, her insides melting to the fiery heat of sensations ricocheting through her as his tongue speared and stroked. Her legs liquefied. And just before the rush of pleasure overtook her, he pulled her to the floor and pressed her to her back.

"Hurry, hurry!" she pleaded, frantically groping for him. The need to join and possess and feel was savage, frenzied, stealing every thought and leaving only untamed passion as she pulled him on top of her, into her arms, spreading her thighs and cradling him between.

Lucas wanted to savor, to taste and touch and give her pleasure she would never forget, but he couldn't hold back.

Fifteen years was a long time to wait.

And when she shoved his jeans lower, wrapping her nimble fingers around his arousal and guiding him to the wet warmth of her softness, Lucas lost it. He entered her fully in one hard stroke, buried deep and thick, and she arched off the floor, calling his name in a way he'd never heard before. Deep and throaty. Utterly erotic.

He withdrew and shoved deeply, sheathing himself, coming home with every measured hot stroke. And Angela wanted more, her hips rising to greet his, to urge him on. All she could think of was that she was finally with him, that her heart was beating in sync with his, and instinct and knowledge melted. They were a perfect match. Without ever knowing each other's needs, they touched and tasted and pulsed with a sweet hot rhythm of desire.

The roughness of him slid smoothly into her, and she welcomed him, her body pawing for his return. Impatient desire spread and throbbed.

His pace quickened, and she joined the tempo.

His arms braced, he captured her head between his palms, his gaze locked with her as he loved her. "I've wanted you forever."

"Oh, me, too, me, too." Tears glossed her eyes.

He withdrew completely and plunged, and she gasped and moaned her pleasure, kissing him again and again.

"Ah, Angel, you feel so good, so perfect."

"Lucas, Oh, Lucas…more, more—I—"

"I know, baby, I know. I can feel it. I feel everything about you. *Everything*." As if he'd made love to her for years, he was attuned to her body, to the flex of feminine muscles, to the heavy throbbing in his groin that fought against explosion he barely held in check.

Her body tightened, her breathing skipped, and he continued to claim her, pushing her higher, further. Quick and hungry.

It was raw and primal. Erotic. Pulsing. The power of their cadence driving them across the carpet. He shoved once more, grinding into her, and passion erupted. Blood rushed hotly in his veins as he convulsed with a rapture so pure and complete, it stole his breath.

Angela felt him throb inside her, elongate and pulse as pleasure ripped and tore through her, joining with his. She bowed beneath him, digging her heels into the carpet and pulling him harder into her body as it gripped and flexed with a heated climax that shattered her soul.

They remained suspended for a few seconds, straining, the peak of desire slipping over the edge into bliss. Angela opened her eyes, gazing at him, struggling for air, her body satisfied but not sated. She never would be, she thought, and touched his face, seeing him as she had in her dreams. He nipped her fingers and sank down onto her, kissing her again and again, as if he was afraid she'd disappear.

For long moments they held each other, her legs locked around him, his arms trapping her. Lucas squeezed his eyes shut, feeling complete and whole for the first time in his life. He'd been like a thirsty man running toward water. Nothing could have stopped this. From the moment his mouth touched hers, he never wanted it to end. He still didn't. A clear, piercing possession reared in him as he ground his mouth against the bend of her throat. She was his. Finally.

Angela moaned, trying to catch her breath, her hands smoothing over his muscled back.

Then it hit her. Really hit her what they had done.

She'd made love with her best friend. Her truest friend.

And it was incredible!

"Oh, Lucas, what have we done?"

Slowly he lifted his head, kissing her once before meeting her gaze. He realized it was the first time he'd made love to a woman without protection. *Worry later,* he thought, for it all seemed insignificant to easing the guilt underlying her voice. "If you don't know, Angel..." He leaned back on his knees, taking her with him. "Then we're gonna do it again."

With her legs wrapped around his hips, he stood and walked to the stairs.

"And again and again."

She smiled, her misgivings slipping away beneath her need to be loved by him. "This might take a while."

"No, Angel, longer, much longer."

Laying her on the bed, he recognized the sudden change in her expression, her concern. "It's done,

Angel. Let's enjoy each other,'' he said, not wanting to hear the reasons they were both pushing to the back of their minds. Not wanting to know that they'd changed their relationship forever and what daylight would bring. Lucas pushed the world aside, stripped off his jeans and sought his darkest desire.

Angela. In his arms, her soft eyes filled with passion.

As he came to her naked and muscled, she laid her hand to his chest. ''I want to, so badly, but have we ruined everything?'' Her gaze searched his as he hovered above her.

Lucas's brow tightened. ''Ruined? Do you think I've been hanging around you for fifteen years so I could get you into my bed?''

She smiled. ''No. But how do you explain this?'' She waved sluggishly to their naked bodies.

''A long time in coming.''

He flashed her a wolfish grin.

''How are we going to deal with this? I mean, people have thought of us as purely platonic friends.''

''I don't care what anyone else thinks, only what you think.'' He held his breath.

''Platonic was hard,'' she admitted, her thumb rasping over his nipple, and his breath hissed out between clenched teeth.

''Darlin', you don't know the meaning of the word hard.'' He laid down on her, his knee insinuating erotically between her thighs, spreading her wide.

''Yes, I do.'' She wrapped her hand around his erection, and Lucas trembled.

Then he kissed her. A deep consuming kiss that had her arching off the bed to get closer to him.

"Tell me that's platonic," he breathed against her lips. "Everything between us is stronger now, Angel. Now hush up and let me make love to you."

And he did.

When logic told her to protest, he kissed her throat, the simple touch melting her bones. When her mind screamed that they'd made love without protection and the consequences would be grave, he closed his lips around her nipple and drew deeply, sending a divine tingling radiating through her blood. He assassinated her senses. Never giving her a chance to draw a breath before another crowded on the last. It was as if Lucas knew what would drive her wild, knew what made her gasp for her next breath. And he knew where she was ticklish and played over her sensitive hip till she screamed and laughed for him to stop.

"You've been driving me nuts for fifteen years," he said against her muscled thigh. "From the instant I saw you in that dorky cheerleading uniform."

"It wasn't dorky, it was cute."

"No, you were cute in it."

Angela smiled as his mouth floated over her flesh, his hands rubbing, caressing, then he slid off the bed and pulled her to the edge. She sat up, but he pushed her down, spread her thighs wide and covered her softness with his mouth.

She came off the bed. "Lucas!"

He chuckled darkly, imprisoning her as his lips and tongue stroked her into reckless pleasure. He adored her gasps and cries and how she held him to her, moaning his name.

His name.

She grappled for him, pulling him off the floor and onto the bed.

"Now, Lucas." Impatience marked her moves as she urged him closer. "Now."

Reaching for the nightstand drawer, he paused to kiss her. "Please tell me you have condoms." He blindly groped for the square foils.

"It's a little late, isn't it?" She wrapped his arousal, stroking him.

He choked. "It's never too late, Angel," he said, dropping a handful of protection onto the bed.

She grabbed a condom and watched his face as she rolled it down. Lucas thought he'd come apart right then. Then she shoved him on his back and straddled his thighs.

Lucas watched the most erotic vision as she guided him deep into her body. "Oh, sweet heaven!" he groaned, slamming his eye shut. "Don't move."

"I can't."

"Baby, please." He rose up and met her gaze. They were nearly nose to nose, his hands cupping her breasts, thumbs circling her nipples.

"Be still," he whispered.

"You don't ask much, do you?"

He smiled tenderly. "I can feel your body holding me tighter and tighter. It's like wet velvet wrapping me."

She didn't blush as she closed her arms around his

neck and kissed him. Still he held her. "I want to move, Luc."

"I know." He grinned. He reached between their bodies and stroked the bead of her sex, one hand keeping her still when she was wont to squirm.

"Lucas," she said on a breathy rasp. "This is torture."

"I know," he said, chuckling when she pushed against him. Lucas loved it, had dreamed of a moment like this. "I knew we'd be good together baby, I knew it."

Then she moved, long measured thrusts against him, her words repaying his torture. "I feel every inch of you," she whispered, then told him how he made her feel—in detail.

And her throaty words stole his control. He tossed her on her back and pushed, taking her with him on the passionate journey neither could stop. She held his gaze, memorizing the sharpness of his features, the softness of his blue eyes as she held him inside.

Her pulse quickened with their pace, her body thrumming like a war drum toward a tingling crescendo.

"Lucas," she cried out softly as she joined him, their bodies blending with the beat of their hearts. As the throb of desire continued to ripple through her, Angela knew she'd lost the battle with her very soul.

She loved Lucas like a woman loves a man. She always had. She just didn't dare believe it before. He was the best part of her life. The only man she wanted in it. Her throat closed when she thought of the future, but the feel of him making love to her, his hard warmth, obliterated the thought as he took her on the wild rush to heaven and let her find it in his arms.

Angela rolled over and found her bed empty. She sat up sharply, an odd panic sweeping her until she heard the shower running. The scent of coffee filled the room, and she found a cup on the bedside table, still steaming. Beside two aspirin. Her head didn't hurt much, but she took them anyway with a sip of coffee, listening to Lucas hum over the sound of the running water. Yet her gaze kept falling on the rumpled sheets, the empty condom wrappers.

"Oh, Lord," she groaned, giving up counting them. Mercy, she would never look at her kitchen table again without thinking of him licking strawberry jam off her breasts, then making love to her on the cool floor. They'd explored and learned each other. In one night they'd gone from buddies to lovers. And it was the most incredible, powerful sex she'd ever had. Heck, she'd known Lucas was a lady's man simply by his reputation with women, and secretly she admitted she'd been jealous that women who were unworthy of him received the benefit of his skill.

Oh, man, was he *skilled.*

Her body tingled with the memory, and she squirmed on the bed.

"Mornin', Angel," came a deep husky voice.

She looked up as he strolled from the bathroom in a wake of steam. Long, lean and deliciously danger-ous in only a towel, she thought, growing warm and flushed. His muscles flexed and jumped as he used another towel to dry his hair, and all Angela wanted to do was throw him down on the bed and make love to him again. He'd been hard on her senses before. Now he was complete chaos.

"Good morning," she said.

Lucas read the look in her eyes, the same one he'd seen all night, every time he touched her. It thrilled him, made him want to roar with the knowledge that making love with her wasn't a mistake.

"I hope that smile is because of last night."

"If I say so, then you'll just go and get all arrogant on me." She waved him off. "And you know how I hate arrogant men."

He grinned. "Yeah, you've mentioned that a time or two in the last fifteen years."

She blinked, his words bringing back the fact that years of friendship were now permanently altered.

"No, don't regret it," he said, a plea and warning in his tone.

"I don't, but the fact remains, Lucas, we might have had wonderful sex, but we still don't want the same things."

His features turned harsh. She wanted babies, he didn't. "And we did it once without protection."

He seemed to be ignoring her real point. The lack of a future. "Yeah," she said. "That, too."

"Angela, honey," he began, and she didn't like the forgive-me tone he was using. "I want you to know that I—"

His pager went off, the sound blaring reality into the somber bedroom. Lucas muttered a curse and walked to the nightstand. "I just told them I'd be in, for heaven's sake." He called the hospital, speaking softly, his irritation turning to concern. Hanging up, he faced her. "I have to go."

She nodded.

"I know this isn't the best time, but—"

"I understand, Luc. Believe me."

"Go back to sleep," he said, slipping onto the bed and pulling her into his arms. "Dream of me."

She smiled. "There's that arrogance again."

"No, just hope."

Her smile fell, and she ran her fingers through his damp hair. "We'll have to talk."

"I know, but not now." He checked her eyes, felt the lump on her head that was down considerably.

"So now you see if I'm okay?" she said, falsely appalled.

"Didn't think about that last night when I was licking jam off you, when I was inside you and you were screaming my name."

"I didn't scream."

"Wanna bet?" He slid his hand under the sheets and parted her, his fingertips playing seductively over her flesh. And she called out his name. "Ah, Angel, it feels like I've waited an eternity to hear you say my name like that."

"Okay, you win. You win!" He thrust two fingers inside her— "Oh, *Lucas*." He bent to her breast, taking her nipple deep into the heat of his mouth as his fingers brought her to a quick, shattering climax. She'd barely caught her breath when she reached for the towel. And for him.

He caught her hand. "I have to get to the hospital. Plus run by my place for extra clothes."

"Look in my car. I picked up your dry cleaning yesterday morning."

"That's my good little wife for hire," he said and she punched him playfully.

"Watch it, buster."

Laughing to himself, he left the bed. She watched him pull on his jeans, enjoying the sight of all that man in her bedroom.

Lucas searched for his shirt.

"It's downstairs," she said.

"Probably in shreds."

She blushed and threw a pillow at him. "And please don't let the world see you looking like that."

He looked down at himself, his arousal pressing again the fabric of his jeans. Only his gaze shifted to her, ice-blue eyes beneath a shock of black hair. The look made her hot all over again "I've been in this state for the past two years, Angel. Get used to it."

She blinked, her eyes rounded. Then she smiled like a cat.

"Don't look so pleased. We have a lot of time to make up for."

He leaned down and kissed her, wrapping one arm around her waist and dragging her up to her knees and against him. It was a consuming, possessive kiss, like their first one.

With the same affect.

He drew back, gulping for air. "Whoa."

Angela sank into the bed, and Lucas stared at her, his gaze rolling over her bare skin and committing the vision to memory before he said goodbye. He told her he would call her in a couple of hours, then left.

Angela felt suddenly alone.

But the unspoken words hung in the air.

That no matter how great they were together, no matter how much she loved him, she knew he wouldn't change his mind about children.

Even for her.

And she prayed they hadn't made one in the heat of passion.

Because it was the surest way to lose him.

Eight

Lucas had a job he couldn't rush through when he needed to be somewhere else. And he needed to be with Angela.

He could only imagine what she must be thinking right now. Because he was, frankly, standing her up. They were supposed to have lunch together at Plum's, out on a real date. Angela'd be fighting mad, he thought. Especially since he hadn't had the chance to call since he left her that morning.

His lips curved as he finished making the last stitch in his patient's little thumb, then wrote prescriptions while Sandy bandaged the wound. He could hardly think straight all day, the images of Angela in his arms and taking him into her body throbbing through his blood like hot wine. He only had to think about her bare skin beneath his mouth and he grew hard. It made for a very long day.

"Doctor?"

He shook free from the sensual thought and looked at Sandy. She held out a chart for him to sign. He read the notations she'd made, her handwriting always better than his, then scribbled his signature.

As she escorted the child and his mother out, Lucas headed for the phone on the wall. He never made it.

"Oh, no, not yet, Dr. Ryder. Joey Marsh is waiting."

Lucas groaned, facing Sandy. "What is it this time?"

"Has a pea up his nose." She tried to hide her smiled and failed.

"Only one?" Lucas laughed softly. "Let's go see if we can calm Mrs. Marsh. That boy must drive her crazy."

They walked from the treatment room down the hall as Sandy spoke softly. "She said if he did it again he was going to spend the next three years breathing out of his mouth because she threatened to tape his nose shut."

Lucas smiled, knowing Mrs. Marsh never would do it. He glanced at his watch, the phone on the nurse's station, then to the stack of charts and the corridor full of patients waiting for his attention. He just didn't have time to call, he thought, then stepped into his office.

Four hours later, when he finally sank into his chair behind his desk, he dialed Angela's number. He got her machine and left a message. Then he called his own place thinking maybe she was working there, but got his own machine.

Where was she? he wondered. She wasn't due to go on the air for several hours. Was she mad that he hadn't called? Was she avoiding him? The image of her standing right by the phone, listening to the tape, skipped through his mind. *No,* he thought, *don't get worked up.* This was Angela, and she rarely kept quiet when she was mad. Lucas rubbed his hand across his mouth, realizing he felt a little insecure about his relationship with her when he never had before.

With women in his past, sex had made little difference. With Angela, it had changed everything. He could always count on her and know what she was thinking.

Now he couldn't.

Because now, he was afraid of losing her.

When Lucas didn't show up for their date, Angela felt abandoned, her heart bruised till she'd called the hospital and learned he was backed up with patients. Instantly she forgave him, but her own wild thoughts were driving her crazy. So she did her Wife Incorporated job, looking at his place, his things, a little differently this time. Especially his grand four-poster bed.

When she found herself lying in the center of it, inhaling his scent, she knew she needed to get out for some fresh air and a friendly ear to bend. Now she and Katherine Davenport sat at a table for two at a waterfront café. The air was humid, but the sultry breeze coming off the river pushed at her hair, cooling her off. Tourists strolled the wooden walk near the river. Waiters moved around, serving customers.

"I knew it the minute I heard your voice on the phone," Katherine said, then forked a piece of her salad. "You had an excited 'Oh, Lord, what have I done' tone in your voice."

"I want you to explain that to me someday," Angela said, sinking back into her chair. "Sounds like a 'Jeopardy' question."

Kat was right, though. She was thrilled about being with Lucas. Last night had been some of the most satisfying moments of her life. Like finding peace after a lifetime of turmoil. And the powerful need for him just kept growing, smothering her sense with just the thought of lying with him. Yet her happiness lay under a haze of confused feelings that had pelted her all day.

She loved Lucas. There had never been any doubt. He was her soul mate. Always had been. And once she allowed her true feelings to flood in as she'd dreamed, they poured through her and sprouted wings. It was as if she'd been awakened from a long sleep with a single kiss.

And a little more than a kiss, she thought with a private smile.

Yet it also left her feeling uncertain.

For the differences between them were glaring. And she hated that it was over something as joyful as having babies.

"Well?" Kat pestered into her thoughts.

Angela met her gaze. "I won't kiss and tell."

"Sugah, from that smile, looks like y'all did a lot more than kiss."

Angela reddened. "Yeah, well." Suddenly she leaned forward, her voice low. "What am I going to do?"

Katherine looked at her as if she were the village idiot. "Love him, marry him."

She shook her head. "He hasn't asked, and it's too early for that. Besides, we don't want the same future, Kat. If we did, this would have happened a lot sooner."

"Heck, you would have had a brood of black-haired babies by now."

Sudden joy punched her in the chest, and Angela allowed herself to have a fleeting vision of holding Lucas's baby, then it dissolved into reality. "And what if I'm pregnant?"

Kat inhaled a sharp breath, and Angela read the question in her eyes.

"Only once."

"That's all it takes."

Angela made a sour face, a tinge of fear skating up her spine. "Hush up, I don't need to think about that right now." It wasn't her most fertile time, she thought, then remembered what he'd said when he'd hunted down protection. *It's never too late.* It proved to her what he'd been saying all along. No kids. Not even by accident.

"Oh, yes, Katie Scarlett O'Hara, tomorrow is another day. That helps a lot right now." Abruptly Katherine set down her fork. "Oh, Lord, you're still going through with it."

It. Artificial insemination. "Yes." Her voice lacked a bit of confidence, she noticed.

"How can you do that when your relationship with Lucas has changed?"

"Because if I don't do what I want, then it will never be a real relationship. I will regret it if I married him and didn't have children because he didn't want them."

"He could change his mind after marriage," Kat said.

"I'd end up resenting him and he'd feel guilty. I don't want him that way."

"I think you need to be talking to him."

"I 'spect there will be more yelling than talk."

"You're asking for trouble. Everything has changed between you two. Why wouldn't this change for him, too?"

She shook her head. "Not Lucas. I know him." He was so dead set against it Angela was surprised he hadn't had a vasectomy to prove it. "Unfortunately, the only baby I want to have is his, and he won't give it to me."

So why then, she wondered, was she even considering going through with this procedure?

A school bus accident kept him busy. Lucas never left the hospital, and even when her misgivings were on the rise, Angela packed a lunch and fresh clothes, leaving the bundle with Sandy because he was in ICU with the injured children.

A week passed before they spoke more than ten words to each other, and Angela wondered if he could

hear the longing in her voice. The need to see him.
Feel his arms around her. For him to tell her that they
hadn't made a mistake last week.

God, she hated feeling this way. So uncertain.

Especially when in her heart she knew they were
headed for trouble.

And it found her when she was cleaning his bathroom and he appeared in the doorway.

"Hi."

She looked up as she shut the water off, her heart
skipping a beat. "Hey, yourself, Doc. You look exhausted." Though his suit jacket was crisp, his trousers and shirt were hopelessly wrinkled.

"You look great." Lucas's gaze moved over her,
the cropped white T-shirt and Capri slacks doing
wonderful things to his mood. He stepped into the
bathroom and drew her into his arms. Instantly the
tension and the exhaustion of the past few days
slipped away. She was so much of a safe harbor in
his life that Lucas wondered what he'd do without
her. "Thanks for the meal and fresh clothes," he said.

"You're welcome," Angela whispered, running
her hands over the back of his head and closing her
eyes. *Oh, this feels so wonderful,* she thought, and
squeezed him tighter.

"I've missed you, Angel," he murmured, then
kissed her.

It was instantaneous, like the first time, a hard pull
of emotion and desire, and Lucas understood that it
would always be like this, and he tightened his arms
around her, lifting her off the floor and stepping out
of the bathroom. He didn't stop as he set her on her

feet, his hands seeking her skin beneath her T-shirt, and a bolt of pure lust shot through him when he realized she wasn't wearing a bra. He filled his palms with her soft, rounded flesh.

Angela gasped against his lips, pushing into his warm touch, loving the hard rush of desire slamming into her body.

"God, I missed you," he said hoarsely. "I missed touching you. You're all I've thought about."

"Liar," she said breathlessly as his thumbs pressed and circled her nipple. "You were working, and nothing breaks through that."

"You do." His mouth trailed lower. "You do," he said, pushing up her shirt and closing his lips tightly around her nipple.

She whispered his name, and he bent her back over his arm, laving harder.

"I want you. Oh, Ange, I need you so badly." His free hand mapped her body from thigh to breast, eliciting soft moans. He backed her up against the nearest wall and ground his body to her, insinuating his knee between hers.

Angela answered the erotic pressure, rocking, her body damp and ready for him. She wanted him right now and knew if they didn't stop, they'd be on the floor naked and rolling in a second.

"Lucas," she said, trying to find the strength to stop. Oh, but it felt so good… "Lucas. We have to stop."

"Says who?"

"Me."

He stilled, his brows drawing down as he straightened. "Why?"

She touched his cheek. "Well, for one, I have to be on the air in two hours and have to go home to shower and change."

"That's two hours. Come to bed with me and shower here." He grasped her hand and pulled her down the hall toward his bedroom.

She dug her heels in when she wanted to leap on him right now. But they had to talk, had to work this problem out. Even though she knew it was hopeless. "My clothes are at home, and I have to finish cleaning this place."

He stopped and faced her. But she was already walking into the living room. He darted forward and caught her hand, spinning her around and scowling. "What's with you?"

She shrugged. "Gee, I don't know. Maybe its because I slept with my best friend."

He stepped closer, his voice low and rough. "You made love with your best friend."

Her heart skipped to her throat. "Yeah," she said on a smile. "But how are we going to deal with this?"

"This? We are dealing with it. And there is nothing to moan over, Ange. We just look at each other differently." His velvety gaze swept her. "Like when you're naked and panting."

A fresh burst of desire pulsed up the back of her thighs. She ignored it and said what was on her mind. "Lucas, honey. Where is this leading?"

He knew what she was asking, what point she was

driving home, and his expression darkened. "I don't want children Ange, you know that. For pity's sake, I just put five back together."

"And this stops you from wanting them, huh?"

"No, it's the fact that I'd be lousy at it. I don't have the skills for it."

"You're cheating yourself, Luc. But I can't be the one to convince you. You have to want it like I do."

He stared at her for a moment, then his features pulled taut. "You aren't still thinking about artificial insemination, are you?"

"Yes, as a matter of fact I'm—"

"No!"

She blinked at his harsh tone. "Lucas—"

"No, Angela. Absolutely not. God, the thought of it chills me. A strange man's baby inside you—"

She'd rather have his baby, but that sure wasn't going to happen. "Dammit, Lucas. That's the only way I will have one! And just because we had sex doesn't give you the right to tell me what to do. And neither would marriage."

Angered, he snapped, "And neither will marriage change my mind about children, either."

She inhaled. Hearing the words hurt even more. Their impasse stung deeply. "I know, and even if you did, Ryder, it still wouldn't change the fact that I make decisions with my body myself!"

He opened his mouth, then slammed it shut. She was right, of course, and he cursed the ugly jealousy and anger running through his blood right now. He didn't want to lose her. God, he couldn't. But he could see their relationship decaying before his eyes. His chest tightened, and he reached for her.

She stepped back. "Do you think I would have suddenly dropped my dreams in the trash because we've made love?"

"Well, no, but I…well…" He raked his fingers through his hair, then burst out, "Hell, yes, if you want to know the truth. Everything is different. We have each other now, Ange."

"And I want babies."

"I'm not enough for you?"

He sounded so wounded, and her expression fell. She rushed to him, gripping his upper arms and forcing him to look her in the eye. "Oh, darlin', that's not it. I…I love you, Lucas." He swallowed visibly, his gaze searching hers. "I always have. Now more than ever." Tears filled her eyes, her heart slowly shattering when he didn't respond, didn't say the words she longed to hear from him. "I want a life with you, but…you would grow to hate me."

"I could never do that."

"Even if we made a future, I would still feel this emptiness, this need to hold my own child. And I would resent you for denying me that. And you would hate me for wanting a… God—" she closed her eyes briefly, her fingers tightening on his arms "—oh, this hurts."

Her voice broke, and when she tried to pull away, he grabbed her.

"But we can't have a future, Luc. We want different lives."

Panic assailed him like a storm. Hard and unforgiving. "Ange, baby, don't talk like this."

"It was a mistake to cross the line, Luc."

"No, it was the best thing to happen to us! Nothing is settled, but my Lord, I feel you slipping away from me."

She lifted her gaze to his, her throat choking off her words. "I can't talk anymore." She pushed out of his arms.

Lucas reached for her, grasping air. "Baby, we need to talk about this more. We do." He followed her as she hurried to the door. "God, don't leave like this."

She looked at him, tears trickling hopelessly down her cheeks. "I don't want to hurt you, Luc. But if the man I love won't give me a baby, then a man I don't know will."

She was out the door before he could call to her.

Lucas fell back against the door, his throat working over and over to keep the knot of agony from strangling him. His chest was stiff and tight, and he realized this time, he knew what real heartache felt like.

And it was killing him.

Angela sat in the doctor's office, waiting for her physician to return with the final test results. They had to screen her for disease, blood levels and a half dozen other things she wasn't concerned with right now before they did the first procedure. Today. She had enough money and she knew if she waited, Lucas would find a way to talk her out of it. And she would grow to resent him.

She couldn't bear that.

Nor was she hoping that once she was pregnant he would change his mind. It would be false hope. She was too old to be hanging onto that.

He hadn't called since she left his place last week. But then, neither had she. It hurt, their fight, her need for him that went unanswered. She could hardly think of him without feeling as if her chest was caving in. Her mom had noticed and asked if she was ill. Even her sisters questioned her, though she'd confided her plan of artificial insemination only to Sarah weeks ago. Her sister was supportive, but Angela knew she hadn't approved. But what did Sarah know? She was happily married and already had three kids.

Angela felt like the spinster grasping for a life she never got. Suddenly Lucas's face loomed in her mind, and she wondered if she was prepared to lose him over this. Lose her best friend, her love. Seconds ticked by, and she decided that she wouldn't do this procedure, not right now. It was rash, too knee-jerk, especially when her heart was aching so badly. She had to talk with Lucas again, though she didn't know what she would say. She knew she couldn't go another moment without considering the man she loved. Lucas came first.

Grabbing her handbag, she stood and was about to write a note for her doctor when the door opened. Carrying a chart, the physician smiled, then crossed to her desk and propped her rear on the edge.

Angela frowned at the blond-haired woman who looked too young to be a physician anyway, let alone a specialist. "I was just leaving. I've decided to postpone this for a few weeks."

The doctor nodded, then glanced at the chart in her hand. "You might want to postpone this for a little while longer."

The doctor wore an odd smile that made Angela nervous. What did they find? "How long?"

"About eight months."

Angela swallowed, dread washing over her like a mountain of heavy stones. "I beg your pardon?" No, *no!*

"You're already pregnant, Miss Justice. About three weeks, according to your hormone levels."

Three weeks.

Lucas.

Oh, God.

She dropped into the chair.

Life was just getting too cruel.

She had the baby she wanted, from a man who didn't want to be a father.

Nine

Angela staggered from the bathroom and carefully crawled onto the bed, praying that was her last bout of morning sickness. Even though it was one in the afternoon. Her child, it seemed, had her timing down according to Angela's crazy nighttime schedule. She got in at five-thirty in the morning, slept till noon then wretched her guts out for the next hour. What a way to start a day, she thought rolling to her back.

She covered her abdomen, closing her eyes and silently asking her child to go back to sleep. It felt as if the instant she'd learned she was pregnant all the symptoms started battering her.

The phone rang, but she let the machine pick it up. She couldn't form a coherent sentence right now, anyway. Then she heard Lucas's voice, and everything in her jumped back to life.

"Angel, call me. I can't stand this. It's been too long. I need you."

I need you.

Not I love you, I can't live without you... She closed her eyes, unable to face him just yet. She was still trying to get used to the idea of finally being pregnant. With Luc's baby. A baby he didn't want.

And she knew what would happen once he knew.

He'd push her away as he'd done with every other woman in his life. His commitment phobia was part of this, she thought. Fatherhood would force him. And she didn't want him like that. She wanted...she wanted it all.

No use putting this off, she thought, and sat up sharply. The motion was a mistake. Another wave of nausea hit, and she swallowed, reaching for the glass of water on the nightstand. She drank and put her head down, waiting for the sensation to pass, her mind filled with Lucas.

Always Lucas.

Her heart ached. Her body yearned for him.

She moaned and set the glass aside, cradling her head in her hands.

She had to tell him.

Today.

Lucas was glad it was the weekend and he wasn't on call. His bedside manner had been lousy all week, and the kids didn't deserve it. He needed to be alone. Except all this aloneness was driving him nuts. Slumped in his couch, he channel surfed, a mug of coffee in his fist. Even cartoons didn't interest him.

A first. Finally he shut off the TV and sighed deeper into the couch. He hadn't even wanted to get up this morning. Facing another day without a glimpse of Angela was eating him alive.

He'd listened to her on the radio every night since she'd left him. Just hearing her voice soothed him, and he wondered if she was as unhappy as he was.

The phone rang, and he heard her voice through the machine. Lucas leaped toward the phone, grabbing the receiver. "Angel?" His heart thundered hard in his chest.

"Hey, medicine man. How are you?" On the other end of the line Angela squeezed her eyes shut. Oh, Lord, it was so good to hear his voice again.

Lucas let out a long, satisfied breath. "Lousy. I miss you, Angel."

Her chest clenched. "I miss you, too." She plucked at the hem of her shirt, swallowing thickly.

"Then let me see you. I feel like an addict who's been cut off cold turkey."

The corner of her mouth curved. "Same here." Since he'd been back, this was the longest they'd been apart, and even when he had lived elsewhere, they'd talked a couple of times a week, at least. A part of her was missing when Lucas was away.

"We can work this out, I know we can. Talk to me."

The determination in his voice stung. The only way to work this out was for Lucas to suddenly change his mind about children. "You might not like what I have to say."

"Baby, whatever it is, there's got to be a solution. I can't lose you. I won't."

"Plum's Café, in an hour. Okay?"

He glanced at the clock on the mantel. "I'll be there."

His voice sounded so eager, and Angela tried not to cry. "Okay. Bye."

Lucas hung up, then headed to the bedroom to change out of his sweats. He paused, frowning at the phone. Her voice had sounded cautious, tired.

And a little scared.

Angela rounded the corner between the historic buildings, walking toward the café. She stopped short when she saw Lucas.

In his arms was another woman.

Her heart dropped to her knees. Anger and jealousy filled the empty spot as he smiled at the small blond woman, saying something she couldn't hear. Angela couldn't move. She watched him touch the woman's cheek, smile at her when Angela was feeling rotten down to her toes.

When her heart was breaking in two and lying on the ground at her feet.

She took a step, not willing to let this go, then decided she didn't want to make a scene for the whole town to see. She turned away.

"Angela!" he called.

She kept walking, her steps quickening toward her car.

Lucas rushed after her, and just as she was about

to open the car door, he caught her arm. "Why are you leaving? Didn't you hear me?"

She jammed her key into the lock. "I heard and I saw." She glared at him, her gaze shifting over his shoulder to the woman, then back to him. "I knew you were short on commitment, Lucas, but gee, this has to be a record. Even for you."

"What?" He looked at the blonde, then at her, frowning. "You've got it wrong, honey."

"Do I? I ask you to meet me and I see you with another woman." She pushed open the car door, forcing him to step back.

Lucas grabbed her and pulled her away from the car, suddenly aware of the attention they were drawing. He walked to his car, opened the passenger side and growled, "Get in."

Angela scowled, then climbed into the low-slung Jaguar.

Lucas got in, turned on the engine, the AC, then gripped the steering wheel. "You're jealous."

"Damn right I am."

"You have no reason to be," he said. "And you're the one who pushed me out."

"I know. I didn't want to."

He shot her a hot look. "Then don't."

"You have a reputation I'm well acquainted with, Luc. I've heard about every one of your conquests. What am I supposed to think when I see you holding another woman?"

He leaned over the console and stared hard into her eyes. "You're supposed to trust me. Like you have for fifteen years." Her expression softened with guilt.

"And that was a patient's mother. She was thanking me for saving her son's life."

Angela blinked, her anger melting away. "A patient?"

"Yeah." He shifted closer, his gaze locked on her. "You are the only woman I want to hold, Angel."

Her heart leaped, then fell again as she remembered what she had to tell him. "I'm sorry. It's just that since we've been apart, I can hardly think of anything else and what a mistake we've made."

"No, dammit, we didn't." Then he kissed her.

And the days apart vanished into a hot eruption.

She leaned into him, and he pulled her over the console and against his chest. His mouth was savage on hers, lips and tongue possessing, seducing, showing how much he'd missed her, needed her. They couldn't get close enough fast enough, and his hand was under her blouse, hers roaming over his slacks. Lucas groaned with frustration as she outlined his erection. Abruptly, he set her into the seat and pulled into traffic, the sleek sports car taking the corners like a snake. He shifted gears, his gaze on the road ahead as he slipped his hand under the hem of her skirt, nudging her thighs apart.

"Lucas!"

"Open for me, baby, I need to touch you."

She did, her willpower vanishing, and his fingertips slipped under the fabric of her panties and into the folds of damp flesh. Her breath caught, and she pushed into his touch. He played with an intention she couldn't mistake.

Angela didn't care.

He was touching her, and that was all she could think about. All he let her think about. Thoughts of revealing her secret fled as he stroked her up and down.

"Shift the gear," he said, and she did, not wanting him to stop, and as he pulled into his driveway, into the garage, she was ready to make love to him right then and there.

The closing door sealed them in darkness, and in seconds he was at the passenger side, pulling her from the seat and kissing her again. The cool steel of the Jaguar met the back of her bare thighs, and the sensation rocketed desire through her with hot demand. And Lucas obliged, pushing up her skirt, his thumbs hooking the thin band of her panties and snapping it.

Her shock overrode her desire, and he laid her back over the hood, scooped his hands beneath her buttocks and lifted her. He met her gaze, a crooked, sexy grin curving his lips before he tasted her.

"Lucas!"

He held her tightly to him, his motions devouring and lush, his tongue darting, plunging. Her hips rocked, but he kept her prisoner, torturing her over and over, sucking the bead of her sex and making her arch off the cool metal hood.

Then he parted her and pushed two fingers deep inside her. Angela found paradise instantly, the rip of it driving a scream from her throat and echoing in the dark garage. Her body convulsed wildly, without control, his imprisonment making her pleasure more powerful. He thrust with a determined motion, and when he felt her body calm, he dragged her off the car and pulled her into the house.

"I can't believe you did that to my panties," she said, staggering weakly.

"Yeah, I know," he growled, and once inside pulled her into his arms, kissing her with a ferocity she recognized. "And I need to get you out of these, too, fast." He opened her blouse, unclasped her bra, then filled his palms with her breasts.

She pushed into his touch, driving him backward. "You, too." She worked the buttons of his shirt open as they toed off their shoes. Her blouse and bra fell to the carpet, laying a sensual trail as they stumbled into the hall. As if he couldn't wait, he pushed her against the nearest wall and kissed her. And kissed her.

Desperation riddled him, his need for her, not just her body, driving him insane with want. He wanted her, and for two weeks she'd been shutting him out. He'd never felt more lost and wanted to be found again, in her arms, in her body, to prove to her that they were matched. Parted from her, he was half alive; with her, he was whole and human and he wanted only to hold her, look into her eyes. There he saw his future, a life he'd dreamed of as a kid.

A place to belong.

He wasn't letting go, ever, and as he stripped off his shirt and mashed her to the wall, his kiss told her so. He peeled her skirt down, cupping her buttocks and bringing her hard against him, whispering that he couldn't wait to be inside her, to feel her body cradle him.

"Then we need less clothes." She kicked her skirt aside, then opened his trousers, her moves hurried with the thrill of passion. Her hand closed over him, and he groaned loudly, thrusting into her palm as he rubbed her breasts.

She slid down the wall, taking his trousers with her. Then she wrapped her hand around his arousal and took him into her mouth.

His mind went blank.

He could barely stand, his hands braced on the wall above her as every touch, every pass of her tongue sent him further and further out of control. He knew he was groaning like a wild man, but he couldn't help it.

"Angel, Ange, honey."

She merely strengthened her motions, holding him prisoner to her sweet assault.

He was going to lose it. And he gripped her under the arms, yanking her upright. He was on her in an instant, his kiss devouring her mouth, her breasts.

Wild. Primal.

He backed up, dragging her with him, against him as he added his trousers to the scatter of clothing. Mouths plundered, hands groped with frenzied passion, rediscovering, memorizing.

In his bedroom they didn't stop.

He swiped a foil packet off the dresser, tearing it open as he pressed her against one of the four bedposts. She gave it a fleeting glance, a little niggle of guilt hitting her as he donned it...until he closed his lips around her nipple and drew it into the heat of this mouth.

All thoughts fled in the heat spiraling through her like a rushing river, spreading to her fingers and toes. He trailed kisses down her body, the curve of her hip, pausing to kiss and stroke her softness before turning her around and marking a path over her buttocks, her spine. Angela dropped her head back, clutching the bedpost as his fingers dipped between her thighs. She pushed against him as he played her body like a well-strung violin, drawing her tighter and tighter.

"Lucas, please." She pushed against his arousal.

The moist heat of her sent surges of anticipation through him as she lowered slightly. Open, vulnerable.

Trusting.

He filled her, deep and thick, gripping her hips and slamming his eyes shut. Completion swelled through his being, stealing his breath. A turmoil of emotions melted with passion, and he withdrew, long and heavy. She moaned, almost a purr, and he answered her, throbbing as her delicate muscles went hard, fisting him in a tight glove of desire.

Angela pulsed shamelessly, wanting his boldness, needing him more desperately in this moment than ever before. It wasn't enough; it was too much. She felt as if she were coming apart, the seams of her soul splitting as she rushed to keep them together.

Lucas felt her impatience, the build straining his own muscles, and he clutched her, shoving and shoving and wanting this to never end. Suddenly he withdrew, and her cry of frustration was smothered beneath his mouth as he turned her in his arms and lifted her.

He pushed smoothly home, lowering her to his bed, never breaking tempo, driving, driving. He cocked one leg slightly, braced above her, and smiled into her beautiful eyes.

He thrust hard, and her gasps tumbled into his mouth.

"You're mine, Angel. You always have been," he whispered. "You always will be."

"Yes," she murmured against his mouth. "Yes. Always. Oh, Lucas."

Bodies met and parted.

Opulent waves of pleasure buffeted them with each thrust, and in his ice-blue eyes she saw his heart, read the depths of his soul. And she gave him hers on the lake of wrinkled sheets.

Primal with emotions.

With unbridled passion.

Feminine muscles clamped like a vise, and he surged into her. She gasped for her next breath, the pulse of luxurious ecstasy breaking as she thrust her hips upward and locked her legs around him.

They ground against each other, rocking, rocking, the splintering passion shooting through her, hard and tense and tingling. She watched his pleasure erupt on his features, heard his breath skip and stall. Yet he never broke eye contact, even as he lengthened and throbbed hotly inside her, even as his climax crushed through him and into her.

They shuddered together, a union binding them.

"Angel. Oh, Angel."

"I know, darlin', I know." It stunned her every time he made love with her. The power and need scrambling wildly inside her, sensations folding over one another and rushing for a release that only he could give.

And as they kissed, both clinging with the same desperation, she didn't want this time to end, didn't want reality and the world to enter this bedroom. For it would bring their problems back, and she'd have to reveal the secret kept safely inside her body.

Lucas dozed lazily, smiling to himself. He could hear Angela searching the house for her clothes and cocked one eye toward the door as she walked in. She was wearing his shirt and looked incredibly sexy in it.

She threw his slacks at him. "I haven't any panties."

He grinned. She looked so cute, her hands on her hips, his shirt open and exposing the cleft between her breasts and the soft curls between her thighs. Why did she bother? "Didn't I tell you it was my fantasy to leave you pantyless when you're around me?"

"What difference do they make since you have me out of them so quickly?"

He chuckled. "Then don't wear any, ever."

She eyed him as she snapped out her skirt, frowning at the wrinkles. "I'm going to look like the town tramp going home like this."

"No, you're not. You're going to look like a woman who's been loved all afternoon." He patted the space beside him. "Stay."

She didn't look at him, shaking her head as she inspected her blouse, which was only slightly less wrinkled. "I have to go into work early and do some promo spots for a new sponsor." Stripping naked, she put on her bra, then her blouse,

Lucas noticed her hands were shaking as she stepped into her skirt. And that she wouldn't look at him.

"Angel?" He left the bed, pulling on his chinos before he crossed to her.

"Yeah?" She zipped her skirt, tucked in her blouse.

Then he remembered how this day had started, with them talking out their problems. He stepped close, tucking two fingers under her chin and forcing her to look him in the eye. "Talk, Ange. I can feel something bottled up inside you."

Angela knew this was the moment she'd dreaded. "I was supposed to have the first procedure this week."

His features tightened. "I take it you didn't?"

She shook her head.

He knew how badly she'd wanted this, and something awful slithered through him just then. "How come?"

"I'd changed my mind. Amazing, huh?" She laughed shortly, and Lucas didn't hear a bit of humor in her tone. "After all my talk I couldn't do it, not at the risk of losing you."

Lucas was at once pleased and sad. He was keeping her from having what she desired because of his desire not to be a father.

"I want a life with you, Lucas, and if I'd gone through with it, I knew I'd lose you."

"Aw, baby, you wouldn't. Nothing is going to stop us from being together. We just have to find a solution."

His earnest tone broke her heart, and she looked away. "I had hoped so."

He frowned. "There's something else you're not saying, I can feel it." She lifted her gaze to his, and the sorrow he saw there kicked him in the chest. "Tell me. My God, you look as if someone is dying."

"When the doctor came into the office with the routine test results, I'd already made up my mind. I was leaving to come see you." His expression said he believed her. "Then she gave me the test results and—" she held her breath, then burst with "—it was too late. I'm already pregnant."

He stared at her as her words sank in. "Pregnant? But if you didn't have the procedure then..." His features went slack.

"*We* made this baby, Lucas." She swallowed. "This child is yours."

Ten

A half dozen emotions passed over his features. Shock, wonder, pleasure, then fear.

"Oh, God."

"Well, that wasn't the reaction I was hoping for," she said, "but it was the one I expected."

That rankled him. "How long have you known?"

"A couple of days."

"And you didn't think to tell me!" he raged.

"I am telling you now, and it took a while for me to get used to the idea, too, you know."

"With anything else you would have come to me instantly."

"Sure, but not when I knew how you felt. You don't want this baby."

He met her gaze. A fist tightened around his heart. "That's not true."

"Really?"

"I want you, and the baby comes with you."

Want you? When would he ever admit he loved her? "Well, duh, there's a stretch."

"Damn, Ange. Give me a second." He pushed his fingers through his hair. "It's not every day a man hears those words."

"And you were hoping never to hear them, I know that."

Tears glossed her eyes, and Lucas felt slayed where he stood. "What's done is done. We'll get married right away."

"The hell we will."

He blinked, shocked, then recovered. "Why the hell not?"

She scoffed. "I'm not marrying you because of a baby, Lucas. I had planned all along to raise my child alone."

"Our child." His eyes narrowed. "So I don't matter? All you care about is this baby?"

"How can you ask that? I wouldn't be feeling torn in half if I didn't love you so much. For heaven's sake, Lucas, the only child I ever wanted was yours but I knew how you felt. It's the reason I never wanted to cross the line with you all these years. I valued your friendship more than my needs. And I, at least, remembered every time you said you didn't want to be a father."

"Dammit, Ange. You've got to marry me. Think of your parents, your sisters and brothers."

"I am thinking of all of us. And I don't want you because of guilt or obligation."

"It's kind of hard to get around those points, you know." He wished the words back the instant they left his lips.

Her brows shot up, hurt clear in her eyes. "Exactly," she said, and her voice broke.

It killed him to hear it. "Aw, honey, listen to me," he said, gripping her shoulders when she tried to move away. "I'm not sorry we've made love, Ange. I don't regret a second of being with you."

"Oh, Lucas," she moaned. "I don't, either, only that it's brought us to this. And it looks pretty grim from my point of view."

"It's not. I want to marry you."

She shook her head. "You'd be doing it because you feel you have to, not because you want to. I don't want that for us. I'll be just fine on my own."

"That's my child inside you." A little burst of joy skipped through him at his own words, surprising him to the core. "I have rights."

"Possession is nine-tenths of the law." She pulled free and headed for the door.

"Oh, no, you don't." He stopped her.

Angela batted at his hands. "No, don't touch me."

He wrapped his arms around her anyway, holding her till she stopped squirming. "We can't be enemies over this, Ange. I won't let it happen." She moaned and sank further into his embrace. "Now, why won't you marry me? Be honest."

Her forehead pressed to his chest, she muttered, "Because you've never been committed to anything in your life except medicine. I've seen proof."

That was problem number what? Four? Five, he thought. "And if I said I wanted this baby?"

She looked up, shoving out of his arms. "Oh, that is the biggest lie of all. For fifteen years you've been telling me you don't want to be a father, Lucas." She paused thoughtfully, then asked, "But if you were so all-fired determined not to be a dad, why didn't you have a vasectomy?"

Lucas stammered, unsure himself, but Angela went on without stopping.

"I'll tell you why. Because somewhere deep inside you, you did want a child. And that scares the hell out of you."

Lucas stood rock still, feeling like she'd just hit him dead in the face. Why *hadn't* he done something permanent? Then he looked at her and knew why. Hope. A thread of hope. But the words wouldn't come off his tongue.

"You don't have to be in this child's life and risk that you just might abandon him," she said sarcastically. "Abandon us." Her voice faltered and her lower lip trembled. "And you don't have to tell anyone you're the father, either. My sister Sarah is the only one in the family who knows that I was going to be artificially inseminated. I can just tell the rest of them that."

Anger crushed over his spine and exploded in his features. "You don't think I wouldn't admit to my own child! Damn you, Angela. Since when have you thought so little of me?"

Hurt shone in his eyes, and Angela's heart cracked

all over again. But the truth spilled easily. "Since I knew I was the only one in love in this relationship."

She walked out. Again. Lucas stared at the empty doorway for a second, then bolted after her. She was in the garage, the door rising, the engine to his car revving.

He rushed to the side of the car. "Ange, wait..."

"No, Lucas," she said over hard, gut-wrenching sobs. She wouldn't even look at him. Then she stepped on the gas and gunned out of his driveway. Lucas watched as she made the corner like a pro, then glanced across the street as his neighbors gawked at the barefoot, bare-chested doctor.

He went into the kitchen and fell into the nearest stool, cradling his head.

He was going to be a father.

He wasn't angry, just shocked, more so that she didn't want him to tell anyone and that she was trying to cut him out. Well, hell, he thought, she knew better than anyone how scared he'd been that he'd turn out like his parents. But he'd stuck with her, and if she thought he was going to accept this "I can do this alone" garbage, she was in for a big surprise.

Possession might be nine-tenths of the law, but a father had rights.

As soon as that thought passed through his mind, he groaned, pushing his fingers through his hair. He didn't want to fight with her. Nor be her adversary. She was having his baby, for heaven's sake. Their baby. And he might not have wanted to be a father, but what was done was done. They were going to be parents, a mom and dad.

Angela would have no trouble being a great mother, but the only fathers he'd ever known well were her brothers and her father, Evan. What would her parents say? He was the favored friend of the family, but was he good enough for their daughter? He had a checkered past and no lineage to speak of. And they all knew he didn't hang around relationships for long.

And what about her father, Evan? Lucas hated to disappoint the one man he respected above all others.

Lord, he thought. Her brothers were going to kill him.

Lucas rarely worked in the well-baby clinic, but he felt compelled to be here. He loved kids, all of them. Maybe too much, he thought. But inside he felt as if he were incapable of anything more than medical attention and bedside manner. Which had been sadly lacking in the last three weeks.

Lucas held the infant close to his chest as he brought her to her mother. "She's in perfect health," he said, laying the baby in her mother's arms.

The father stood behind her and sighed audibly. "Thank God. We'd waited so long to have her."

The new father met his wife's gaze and laid his hand on her shoulder.

The look that passed between them was familiar to Lucas in that he'd seen it often, yet he couldn't quite grasp the meaning behind it until now. They'd made a child out of their love. Wanted the baby in their lives. And he wondered what his life would have been like if his parents had wanted him. Suddenly an old memory pierced his thoughts. Him, standing on the steps of the school, a backpack slung over his shoulder, and at the time he hadn't known it had been filled with his clothes. The instant he'd looked inside to get his papers and pencil for class, he'd known his mother wasn't coming back. He'd agonized all day about where he would go, where he could hide so people didn't know that his mother hadn't loved him enough to want him in her life. And the feeling of worthlessness and abandonment had clung till Angela had walked into his life.

He pinched the bridge of his nose, exhaling a long breath as the little family thanked him and packed up the diaper bag. Just as they managed the jumble of strollers and bags, Lucas's gaze fell again on the infant girl. She was a beautiful creation of parents who loved each other. How lucky for her, he thought as the family left.

And what would the state of his life leave for his and Angela's child?

The thought of becoming a father scared the hell out of him, and yet, at the same time, filled him with a joy he'd never known before. He'd spent the past weeks looking at each child that came into his office a little differently, and his nights were tormented with the idea of Angela disappearing from his life and his child never knowing him, never knowing he'd been loved. *Oh, be honest,* he thought. He wanted to be the only one in her life, and he wasn't willing to share. His mother had found something better than him and had taken off like a bat out of hell. He knew in his heart that Angela would never do that. But he was afraid he would. Sticking to anything except his career and his relationship with Angela was all he'd ever done consistently in his life.

And now she wouldn't see him or talk with him. He'd given her only a day before he'd called her. She thought it was over between them. He knew it was just beginning. Yet after leaving a few phone messages and getting no response, he'd staked himself out on her doorstep at six in the morning, only to look like a complete fool and learn she was at Katherine Davenport's. And Kat, being ever the loyal sorority sister, wouldn't let him talk to her.

That was over three weeks ago. She'd quit doing her Wife Incorporated duties so the closest he'd been to Angela was to hear her voice on the radio every night when he couldn't sleep. Then he couldn't sleep because he was worrying about her and wanting to hold her and tell her he only needed a chance. A chance he knew she wouldn't give him.

It infuriated him that she wouldn't marry him.

And he wondered if she would have, even if she wasn't carrying his child. The thought tortured him.

His charge nurse, Sandy, popped her head in. ''You want some lunch? Alice is going down to the deli on the corner.''

''Yes, that'd be great.'' He handed her some money, enough to buy them all lunch. Maybe it would help his mood.

She stepped inside the office, glancing around. ''Didn't Angela stop in? I just saw her in the OB/GYN.''

Lucas was out the door like a shot, panic simmering through him. Why would she be at the clinic this early in her pregnancy unless something was wrong? He pushed through the double doors, striding to the desk and asking for Joyce, her doctor. The nurse buzzed her office, and a moment later, the older woman stepped into the hall, her brows knitted.

"Lucas, this is a surprise. An emergency?"

"No, no. Was Angela just here?"

"You know I can't tell you that, it's privileged—"

"Let him in, Joyce," he heard Angela call.

Lucas stepped inside and around the curtain. "Angela," he said, and he heard the quiver in his voice.

She lifted her gaze to his, and Lucas felt electrified at the sight of her. Just to look into her eyes again made his spinning emotions settle. All this heartache was worth a moment with her. Suddenly, his mind skipped to the last time he'd seen her and the last words she'd said to him. About being the only one in love in this relationship. It was a lie. She wasn't alone. He was here, had always been here, and in that instant, Lucas recognized what had been inside his heart all these years. He loved her. Truly, madly loved her.

But she wouldn't believe him. Not when she knew everything about him and believed he couldn't love her enough. *But I do,* he thought. *Oh, God, I do.*

His gaze swept her beautifully tormented face, then down over her body. Stretched out on the exam table with paper gowns and sheets covering her, her abdomen was exposed, gel shining on her skin.

The baby.

The doctor came to the side and picked up the sensor. She glanced meaningfully at Lucas, and Angela nodded.

The doctor scanned her tummy. Lucas swallowed, very aware that the ultrasound was normal. But the test was a bit too soon.

"Why so early?"

"I had some bad cramps last night and this morning, Lucas," Angela said, her voice wavering.

His heart dropped to his feet, his eyes going wide. "Spotting?" he asked rushing closer, taking her hand and pulling a stool beneath him.

She shook her head.

He stared into her eyes and wanted to erase the fear he saw blooming there. The problems between them faded with the situation. Their child's life hung in the balance, and he muttered silent prayers that their baby was fine and healthy.

"It's going to be all right," he whispered, and she lifted her gaze to his.

Angela didn't have to think. She knew he meant it. Lucas adored children and spent his entire career fighting to save them. He simply hadn't wanted one of his own.

"There she is," Joyce said. "And everything looks perfect."

They both stared at the screen, watching for movement.

"Thank God," Angela whispered, and heard Luc's long-held breath expel. "How can you make anything out of that?" she added, squeezing Lucas's hand.

It was Lucas who leaned over and pointed. "There." He traced legs and an arm. "And there's the heartbeat.'' He swallowed thickly, and his gaze shot to her. She was smiling, touching the screen.

His child, alive and well. And growing inside Angela.

A fresh bolt of happiness spread through him, and he cupped her face, pressing his forehead to hers. ''She has a heartbeat,'' was all he could manage to say.

''Oh, Lucas.'' Angela choked on her tears, and Joyce wiped off her tummy, then slipped out of the exam room, leaving them alone.

Tears spilled, running down into her hair at her temples. Lucas kissed her softly, tenderly, pulling her upright. He smoothed his hands over her hair, pushing it off her face, then kissed her tears.

''You didn't have to go through this alone,'' he whispered, brushing his mouth over hers and reveling in the feel and scent of her. ''Why didn't you call me?''

''I, ah…'' She fell into his kiss briefly, deeply, then drew back. ''I never wanted to force you into being involved.''

''I *am* involved.'' *I'm in love with you.* He wanted to shout at her but knew that would only shut another door between them right now.

''You know what I mean. I can manage alone.''

''But you don't have to.''

''Yes, Lucas, I do.'' She hopped off the exam table and reached for her clothes.

''For the love of Michael, why are you being so stubborn?''

Her gaze flashed to his. "I don't want to let myself in for more disappointment."

Her words left a bleeding trail across his heart. "Dammit, when could you *not* count on me, huh?" He answered for her. "Not once, Ange. I've always been there for you. I was there in the making of this child, and I'll be there when she arrives." The determination in his voice made her freeze.

"Don't you dare tell anyone."

"You won't have to in a couple of months." As she dressed Lucas noticed the changes in her body, her breasts rounder, heavier, her tummy gaining a slight roundness. He didn't want to miss a moment of this, he realized.

"I'll deal with that then."

God, he wanted to shake some sense into her. "Have you told your parents?"

"Nope. Call me chicken."

She shouldn't have to be scared. She shouldn't have to tell them alone, either. "I'll go with you."

"No. It's best for you if you don't say a word."

"If you think I'm going to let the world think that baby is from a test tube, you're nuts."

She straightened her clothing and grabbed her purse. "Say a word to anyone, Lucas, and I'll never forgive you." She walked across the room and slipped into Joyce's office, closing the door.

Lucas could have sworn he heard Angela sobbing. Angela had grown damned tough on him, and he was wondering exactly how he was going to break through the wall she was rapidly building between them.

They'd been buddies for fifteen years, now lovers,

and he wanted to spend the rest of his life being both. He loved her. God, he loved her so much it hurt to look at her, think about her. But she wouldn't believe him. And there wasn't much on his side to convince her otherwise. He had a past that screamed he wasn't ready for anything like this. But that was then. This was now.

Angela needed him, whether she wanted to admit it or not.

He had to find a way past her stubbornness.

Out in the back yard of her parents' house, the house she grew up in, Angela put on her best smile, her happiest attitude for her father's birthday. And she was happy. Lucas's child was growing inside her, and she loved her baby as much as she loved the father. She kept her spirits up by thinking about what their child might look like. Would she have Luc's hair color or hers? His eyes? She couldn't ignore the fact that she'd be looking into the face of the man she loved every time she looked at her child. But marrying him was just not in the cards.

She couldn't do that to him. Force him to commit when she knew it just wasn't in him. And even though she had planned on artificial insemination and raising a child alone, everything had changed. Everything. Because it was Lucas's baby. And dammit, she and her baby deserved more than a man who was only with them because it was the right thing to do.

"Okay, enough of the downer face, Angela Marie," her mom, Sally, said, shifting Angela's attention to the party. "Your dad managed to survive years of

marriage to me and father to all of you, so let's cel-
ebrate.''

Angela smiled. Her mom had made a big produc-
tion out of her father's sixtieth birthday, beginning
with a barbecue, games and the best cake in town.
And Dad was loving every second of the attention.
He even went so far as to wear a party hat and shoot
silly string at the grandkids.

As the afternoon wore on, though, Angela grew
tired of the questions about Lucas. He wasn't here
because of her, and she felt bad about it. He hadn't
missed this event for fifteen years. He'd even flown
in for the weekend once, just for the occasion.

When the cake was a massacre from kiddie fingers
swiping at frosting and the candles were out, Angela
knew she couldn't put this off any longer. It might be
the only time she had them all together for weeks. It
was time to tell them.

With her family around her, Angela tried to gather
her nerve. ''I've some news.''

Her parents looked at her with expectation.

''A promotion?'' her dad said.

She shook her head.

''A new beau?'' her mom asked, a twinkle in her
eyes.

''Sort of.'' She glanced briefly at Sarah and drew
a long breath. ''I'm going to have a baby.''

There was dead silence. A circle of shocked faces
stared at her, and Angela felt every pair of eyes land
on her like hammers.

''Surprise,'' Angela said with a pitifully weak
smile.

Sarah inched forward and said softly, "So you went and did it, huh?"

"Did what?" her father demanded, pulling off his party hat.

Before Angela could speak, Sarah said, "She was planning on being artificially inseminated."

"Oh, for the love of God," her mother said, dropping into the nearest lawn chair.

"I tried to talk her out of it."

"Why would you do such a thing?" her mother asked.

"She didn't," a voice said from behind, and Angela tensed.

Everyone turned as Lucas strode across the lawn, a package tucked under his arm.

Angela stared at him, a warning in her eyes.

"What do you mean, she didn't?" Sally asked glancing between Lucas and Angela. "Are you pregnant or not, honey?"

"Yes, she is," Lucas said as he stopped directly in front of her, setting the gift for Evan aside. "But she didn't get that way by artificial insemination."

Angela's entire body wrung with anger. "Lucas, don't."

Lucas turned his gaze to the only family he'd ever known and took the risk of his life. Smiling, he said, "She got that way because of me. The baby is mine."

Eleven

"So when is the wedding?" Her father's deep voice rumbled into the sudden silence, and Lucas felt Evan's gaze on him, judging him.

"I've tried. I asked," Lucas said, his gaze locked on Angela. Her eyes were screaming at him, shouting, *How dare you?* and he knew that she was going to be furious for a long time.

Lucas didn't care. He refused to allow her to raise his baby alone. Not while he was around. And he *would* be around. Forever, God willing. Nor would he give her any more chances to push him away. He wasn't like his parents. He would never abandon her. Never abandon his child. It wasn't in him. He'd realized that last night, in the middle of eating dinner alone. A meal she'd prepared for him. He knew he couldn't go another second without doing something. Something drastic. And if she was mad, then so be it. She'd get over it. He knew her well enough to count on that. But the worse thing in his life would be to lose her and live the rest of his days alone.

He was tired of being alone.

"It's about time," Sally said.

Angela looked at her mother, shocked. "What?"

"I said it's about time. We've seen it all along."

"Seen what?" She glanced at her family, ending with her mom.

"The way the two of you stare at each other when you know the other isn't looking. How a conversation doesn't go the limit without you mentioning Lucas."

Beside her Luc grinned.

Then Sarah said, "Took you long enough to wake up and smell the coffee, sister."

Angela shifted her gaze to her sister. "You, too?"

"Yeah." Sarah kept eating her piece of birthday cake. "We've been speculating over it for the past ten years or so. Behind your back, of course." Sarah turned to her brother Blaine, her hand out. "You owe me five bucks."

"You bet on me?" Angela said.

"Hey, it was a sure thing," Sarah said, pocketing the cash.

"You bet against me!" Lucas said to Blaine.

Blaine shrugged. "Angela's always been hard-headed."

"Heck," Ford said to Lucas. "I thought you took her virtue."

"Good grief, Ford. A little short on tact, huh?"

Megan, Jason's wife, said to the oldest Justice son, giving him a sour look. "Maybe that's why you're still single, too."

Lucas laughed shortly. "I wish that were the case, but no."

Angela elbowed him, hard. "Bobby Roy Jensen had that honor," Angela said, something inside her easing at the thought of every member of her family knowing the truth and approving. Sort of.

"Gladys's son?" Sally peeped, stunned. "Oh, Lord, save me from hearing any more of that kind of talk."

"Then I guess you don't want to hear how Luc beat the tar out of him," Marc said, winking at his wife, Sarah.

Angela looked at Lucas. "I liked him."

He smiled thinly. "I didn't."

She scoffed, "Oh, you're one to talk, bad boy with a switchblade."

"I want to know when is the *wedding!*" Evan boomed over the conversation that was getting out of hand and off the subject.

Everyone looked at her father, and Angela noticed the redness climbing up his neck.

"Not soon enough for me, Evan."

"Shut up, Lucas," Angela said, and damn if he didn't grin. "You did this so you would have allies," she murmured.

"Yup."

That grin set her teeth on edge, and she felt as if she were being pelted from all sides. Did they think this was easy? Did they believe because they thought it was a great idea, that made it fine and dandy to just up and marry him? "Well, marriage is forever in my book, and it'll take about that long for me to forgive you." She shoved him back and strode through her family and into the house, slamming the door.

"Excuse me," Luc said, and started to follow her.

"Leave her be, Lucas," Evan said, rising from his chair.

Lucas stilled and frowned at the older man.

"Y'all go on. Party's over," he said to the others, then crooked a finger at Lucas. "Come on, son, we need to chat a bit." He swiped the bottle of twenty-year-old sour mash his daughter had given him and two paper cups off the table.

Lucas nodded, something akin to dread working up his spine as they walked to the far end of the yard to the bench. Evan sat and broke the seal on the bottle, splashing his birthday sour mash into the pair of paper cups.

"Now, tell me why my baby girl won't marry you."

Evan sipped his drink, after handing a cup full to Lucas. He took a conciliatory sip, then sat beside the man he thought of as his father.

"So?" Evan prodded.

"She doesn't want me, Evan."

"She had to want something you had to get pregnant."

Luc smiled to himself. Always blunt as hell, he thought. "Oh, that's no problem, it's me and forever she doesn't trust."

Evan snickered. "Just like a woman. Got what she wants all her life and can't understand why she wants it."

"Well, that's part of it. She doesn't believe I love her."

"Do ya?"

Love Angela? The more Lucas thought about it, felt it, the stronger his love for Angela grew. By the day, by the hour. It was as if his heart were a corked bottle, and once it popped, a never-ending river of it flowed through him. And with it came uncertainty.

"Oh, yes. More than I thought possible."

Evan eyeballed him, not ready to approve of this just yet. "Did you tell her?"

"Well, no. Not recently," he added when Evan scowled. "She wouldn't believe me right now, and hell, Evan, she knows how I feel about her. I mean, we risked a lot when we..." Lucas cleared his throat uncomfortably. "Well, you know."

"Made love?"

Lucas looked him dead in the eye and said, "Yes, sir." He shifted on the bench, propping his arm on the back. "You know about my past, my parents."

Evan nodded.

"Well, I always believed I would turn out just like them. Ange knows this. With every woman I've dated, I've ended the relationship before things got too close, too heavy."

"Before you had the chance to fall in love, you mean," Evan said.

"Yeah." Lucas rubbed his mouth. "Angela made a point of reminding me about it often. She was right,

I did do that. But now I know she was the reason I never let relationships get that far. And now, well, she thinks I want to marry her out of obligation or guilt. And I know it's the morally right thing to do, for all of us. But in my heart, I know it's what I've wanted since the day I met her.'' Lucas leaned forward and sighed back on the bench. ''Except now she isn't giving me the chance. Hell, she barely gives me the time of day.''

''Well, then, son.'' Evan clapped him on the back. ''We'll just sit here till we figure out a way.'' Evan smiled at Lucas's hopeless look. ''Because nothing would make me happier than to walk Angela down the aisle right to you, Lucas.''

A ripple of pleasure rolled through his body, and Luc swallowed the knot crowding his throat. His eyes burned. ''Thank you, Evan.''

Evan grabbed his shoulder, giving it an affectionate squeeze. Then after a moment he said, ''However, I'd rather not do it when she's eight months along with my next grandbaby.''

''Me, too.''

Lucas looked toward the house, wondering if the women of this family were siding with her and about to gang up on him.

Elbow-deep in suds, Angela ignored the females littering the kitchen as she washed the pots and pans. She made enough noise to let them know she wasn't in the mood for talking, especially about Lucas.

But they weren't getting the hint, talking behind her, speculating why she wouldn't marry Lucas.

"Hush!" she shouted over the din of voices. "I won't marry Luc just because I'm pregnant."

"Pregnant with *his* baby, Angela," Sarah said.

Angela looked over her shoulder. "Well, duh, I'd forgotten about that."

Sally glanced at the other women, then slid into a chair. Sarah, Meg and Blaine's wife, Kelly, set the table for coffee, then poured.

"Angela Marie," her mother said. "That pot won't come any cleaner, so quit that and come sit. Now."

Angela let her head drop forward and sighed. Her mother had that "set yourself down and give me your side of the story" tone she had whenever Angela and her sisters had fought. Angela rinsed her hands and snatched a dish towel from Sarah, glaring at her.

Sarah smiled.

"I can still beat you up," Angela growled under her breath.

Sarah laughed, grabbing her shoulders and pushing her into the chair. Meg handed Angela a cup of coffee, whispering that it was decaf.

Sally spoke first. "You feeling okay, honey?"

"Aside from morning sickness at one in the afternoon, yeah."

"Good. Now let's talk about why you won't marry Lucas."

Angela cupped her head, her elbows on the table. "This is between Lucas and me." And when she got him alone, she swore she was going to deck him. "Y'all need to just back off."

"Oh, honey, I haven't even started," her mother warned.

Angela looked up and decided not to fight it. Her mom would pester till she got what she wanted anyway. "Fine, hammer away."

"Do you love him?"

Tears filled her eyes.

Sally had her answer.

Her sisters grew silent.

"Now tell me why you won't marry this man, because in my book, young lady, he's the best there is."

She'd never disagree on that. And just to know he was a few yards away made her want to run to him, feel his arms around her. Even if it was only to argue with him, she needed to be near him. "Mom, would you want a man to marry you out of obligation or guilt?"

"Who says that's why he's asking?"

"I'm pregnant with his child. That about says it all."

"Are you telling me," Sarah said, "that Lucas never mentioned marriage before then?"

"Well, no, he did say he wanted to..." After they'd made love that first night. When she'd tried to leave.

"Well, there you have it," Sarah said, settling back in her chair and cupping her mug.

"No! Lucas never wanted to be a father. Never. Ever since I met him, he's always been glad to be with us, with this family, but he didn't want to be a dad. Heal children, yes. Have some of his own, no. It was the reason I never...pursued more than friendship...." Angela rubbed her face. "I've always wanted kids of my own."

"I know. But did you ever think that maybe he

was just scared then?'' her mom said, taking her hand and holding it.

"Of course he is. But I'm not about to make a mistake by marrying a man who doesn't want to be a father, has avoided marriage like the plague and has never been committed to anything but medicine.''

"People change.''

She pulled free and sniffled. "Yeah, well, I think he's asking because of what you and dad would think if he didn't.''

Her mother gawked. "That's ridiculous.''

"Is it? We're his only family, Mom.''

"No, honey,'' her mom said softly. "You've got his only family growing inside you.''

Angela blinked, then looked away. My God. Why hadn't she thought of that? And if Lucas wanted to be a part of her family, why wouldn't he want to be a part of his own?

Angela pushed up from the table and stepped quickly out the back door. Her father was walking across the yard alone.

"Where's Lucas?''

"Gone.''

"Excuse me?'' Panic jolted through her.

"He went home, I guess. I have to tell you, honey, he didn't look very hopeful.''

"What did you say to him?''

"The truth. That if you were set on doing this alone, then he'd better get used to it.''

One look in her father's eyes told Angela she wasn't getting the whole story. Men. They were as bad as women when it came to sticking together. Her daddy was supposed to be on her side.

Angela groaned, then pushed past him toward the back yard gate, running toward the street. She stopped at the curb in time to see the taillights of Lucas's car shift around a corner. Her heart sank as he sped away.

Why did he leave without saying goodbye? Did he realize he didn't want her? And just what did Daddy say to him?

She returned to the house, grabbed her handbag, kissed her parents goodbye and left.

"I know you've been burned, and you have every right to be cautious," Angela said into the station's microphone a few days later. "But what is your heart telling you about this man?" Even as the words left her mouth she felt as if she were betraying her listeners. Who was she to talk?

"He's a great guy, and I want to trust him. My heart's screaming at me to let him in. You know...share with only him."

"Could you live with yourself if you broke it off permanently?"

There was an audible groan on the other end of the line. "No way. I'd regret it all my life."

Angela felt the same feelings and suspicions pounding in her own heart. "Then you have to weigh giving him your trust, against a lifetime of 'what ifs,'" she said to the caller.

"Yeah, I guess you're right."

"Think about it long and hard, caller, then the right decision will be easy."

"Well, all I really know is that ignoring my heart was making me miserable," the woman said, and Angela heard the smile in her voice. "Thanks."

"Glad I could help." Angela cut the line, then turned a dial, bringing up the intro to a country song. "Thank you for calling, and you're listening to KROC radio, with AJ at Midnight. I'll be here with you till the sun rises over the low country."

Angela tapped a key on the keyboard and nodded to the producer as the soft ballad played over the airwaves. She gripped her head, her elbows braced on the desk. She felt like a hypocrite. Who was she to be giving advice when her life was a complete mess?

God. She missed Lucas. Missed him so much her chest ached at the thought of him and her arms throbbed to hold him. She hadn't the will to call him, for hearing his voice was like a slow kill, tearing her heart in half and making her bleed. But even if they fought, she still wanted to be near him.

And he hadn't called her.

He hadn't come over.

She was beginning to think she'd pushed so hard, he'd done exactly what she'd predicted.

He'd run.

Tears burned her eyes, and when her producer tapped the window, she only lifted a hand in acknowledgment and pressed the phone line. "Hi, this is AJ, what can I help you with tonight?"

Lucas's body reacted to the sound of her voice. Soft, husky, with a southern drawl that made his skin tingle. But he could hear the sadness there. He didn't want to make her miserable. He didn't want to feel this lousy, either, but fighting with her, hearing her deny him was tearing him apart.

Every time she pushed him away, it hurt more and

more till Lucas wondered why he was putting himself through this.

Because he loved her and couldn't live without her.

As Lucas lay stretched out on the sofa, Angela's voice pealed through the speakers, and he closed his eyes, wishing she was here and in his arms instead of on the radio giving advice to the lovesick of the low country.

What about them? What advice did she have for them?

He twisted on the cushions when her voice dropped to an octave he recognized. The way she spoke to him when he was pushing inside her, when her body pulled him back and clamped down on his soul.

His throat tightened.

He was jealous that everyone else was hearing her speak that way.

Lucas pushed his fingers through his hair and gripped his head. He loved her and he knew she loved him. She wouldn't be trying so hard to push him away and let him off the hook with their baby if she didn't.

But the root of it was that she knew him and every detail of his past, and she couldn't shake that he'd been a different man then. And was different now because he'd loved her.

And because of it, she didn't trust him anymore.

Lucas didn't know how to regain her trust. He didn't know what he'd done recently to lose it, either.

His past, it seemed, was forever catching up with him and ruining anything good in his life.

Twelve

Angela walked briskly down the hospital corridor, heading for the elevator. She stopped short when Lucas appeared, seemingly out of nowhere.

Her heart dipped, and her gaze clashed with his. Electricity connected, jumping on a train of emotion and charging full steam ahead. Making her hunger. Making her hands itch to touch him. Making her want to see him smile, feel his body against hers.

He stepped close, his gaze raking over her face before he met her eyes and said, "Hi, baby."

She melted right there. "Hey, medicine man."

His brows knitted as he glanced toward the OB clinic. "Everything okay?"

"Yeah, she just wanted to make sure."

His sigh of relief was audible.

"You left the other night without saying good-bye," she said softly. It was like talking to an intimate stranger, she thought, hating this feeling of walking on eggs.

"I didn't think you wanted to talk to me."

How did they get this far apart, she wondered, and knew it was her fault. "I always want to talk to you, Lucas."

"Yeah, I guess it's just that we never agree, lately." He lifted his hand to touch her face, then let it drop.

Angela felt the loss of it like a cut to her soul.

"You're still mad at me for telling them?"

She shook her head, smiling weakly. "I couldn't lie to them. Or deny you the right, if you wanted it."

Was that hope he heard in her voice? "I do," he said with feeling. "I realized that ganging up on you like that was unfair."

"It's okay. They all think I'm dense as a doorknob for not marrying you."

"This is between you and me, Angel, not them. It's our lives, our baby." Her eyes teared a bit, and he groaned. "God, I wish you could—"

He bit off his words as two women passed them, their bellies beautifully rounded with unborn babies, and Lucas's gaze followed them briefly as they got into the elevator.

"I can't wait to see you like that."

Angela was finding it easier to believe him when he was looking so sincere, yet skepticism pushed words past her lips before she could stop them. "Yeah, right."

His attention shot to her. "Don't start doubting me now, Angel," he said softly, crowding her, advancing until she had little to do but come up against him or step back. As he expected, she held her ground. It felt wonderful to be this close to her again, feel her heat, smell her scent. "Not after all this time."

"How can I not, Luc? A one-eighty-degree turn after fifteen years of hearing the same words, the same adamancy, is so hard to believe."

"I'm the one person you should believe," he said and there was a grinding bite to his tone she didn't mistake. "And believe what I say."

Her breath skipped as he encroached a bit further, but when she started to talk, to deny him again, he snatched her against him and kissed her. A hard press, a demanding, soul-consuming kiss for all to see.

Her response was strong and immediate. Just as powerful, just as throbbing and filled with heat. He crushed her against him, his hands mapping her spine, quick and rough, and penetrating her clothes. He kept kissing her till she weakened in his arms, until Angela couldn't think of anything but being with him, naked and primal.

Then, as the elevator chimed, he stepped back, his expression harsh as he pushed her inside. Angela stumbled slightly, then spun around, meeting his gaze.

Not an ounce of happiness showed in his features. "Never doubt."

"Lucas—" The doors closed in her face.

Lucas stared at them for a minute, then turned toward the ward.

* * *

Angela missed him terribly. And being in his house, cleaning, cooking and working as if her heart weren't torn in half, wasn't helping her heartache. Yet as hard as it was to touch his things, smell his cologne, she needed to be near him. Even if it meant cleaning up after him. At least he was being less and less of a slob, she thought, then wondered if it was conscious, because she was pregnant. He never made mention of her stopping this job because of the trouble they were having, and she kept telling herself she was still here because she needed the extra cash and worked practically by rote now. But it was a lie. Just like the one she kept telling herself every morning, that Lucas wanted to marry her to keep his child from being called illegitimate.

The last time she'd seen him played over and over in her mind. The look in his eyes, the feel of his kiss, forcing her to see that beyond the great sex and friendship there was a wild jumble of emotions and doubts.

She was trying, she swore she was.

She didn't want to do this alone.

She ran the dust cloth over the coffee table, stacked the magazines, fluffed pillows, then arranged the couch cushions. One wouldn't fit properly, and when she dug in the cushions, she found a book, *How To Be a Great Dad.*

Her heart skipped and dropped to her stomach, and with a moan she sank to the couch. The pages were dog-eared, his last spot marked. She opened it and found notes and thoughts jotted in the margins. They were mostly about her. And a couple of name choices.

She put the book under the cushion near the arm where she'd found it and tried to block it out of her mind. But when she went to Luc's bedroom, her senses came alive with memories. His scent lingered in the air. She touched the bedpost, smiling, and her body flushed with the warm memory of their loving. Oh, she missed him, she thought, sighing. She stayed that way, her cheek pressed to the post, her arms around it, till she was nearly in tears.

Then she shook the thought free and went back to cleaning.

Returning to the hall closet for the vacuum, she opened the door. The thing practically fell on her. Pulling it out, she frowned at the large box tucked in the back of the closet. *That's why it fell,* she realized, and switching on the light, tilted her head to read the words printed down the side. A high chair. A little smile slipped over her lips. What was he up to?

Clearly she wasn't meant to find the book, but this? Well, she thought, it *was* hidden by winter coats. Taking the vacuum to his room, she cleaned there, nearly sucking up another book stuck under the bed. A medical book on pregnancy. She shook her head, put it on the nightstand and finished her work, deciding that the guest room could wait another day since it was never used, and that she needed to be out of here before he came home from work.

But she wanted to stay. Even if it meant arguing with him. Even if it meant hurting each other, she needed to see him, touch him. Quelling her thoughts, she turned off the oven, left a note of instructions and slipped out. She could get a couple of hours of rest

before her show tonight, she thought, not really in the
mood to offer advice to the lovelorn.

Not when she'd lost the love of her life.

Two days later, Angela stood in Luc's back yard,
staring at the huge, plain brown cartons. She tipped
her head to read the side of a box. A wood swing set
with a slide and deluxe sandbox. A smile wreathed
her face. Lucas would have a hard time putting that
together. He could stitch a wound and save a life
without thought, but mechanically, he was hopeless,
and she could see him laying out the pieces like in-
struments for surgery. She considered calling her
brothers over to help him, then thought, *Let him do
it.* She knew Lucas. He would give it a try himself
before he'd ask for help. The thought brought her up
short. What was he trying to do here, with the high
chair and the books and now this, she wondered,
walking into his house and out of the heat. If he was
trying to convince her he wanted this baby and was
ready for it, he was succeeding. But he wasn't convincing her that he was ready for marriage.

She walked into the living room and froze. It, too,
was filled with boxes, a dainty crib and dresser in
smooth light wood, a matching changing table, a play-
pen complete with umbrella. And Lord, a car seat,
which was laughable because it wouldn't fit in his
Jaguar.

She didn't know whether to be pleased or angry.
She'd wanted to pick these things out. Well, it *was*
her taste, she thought a second later, running her hand
over the headboard of the crib leaning against the end

of the sofa. Did he think that buying all this would sway her? Or was he thinking to prove he could provide when she couldn't?

No, not Lucas, he was never the one-upmanship type.

She went to the kitchen to start dinner, and when she had the pot roast tucked in the warm oven, she headed to the bedroom. She was dusting when she realized there was another dresser in the bedroom, and a vanity. Both matching his set.

Okay, this is big guns, she thought, smiling and peeking in all the drawers of the vanity, sitting for a second on the delicate stool. Shaking her head, she finished in the master bedroom, then headed for the guest room. It was locked. She frowned, flipping through her set of keys for one that might open it. He'd never locked it before.

What didn't he want her to see?

She tried the keys and jiggled the doorknob.

"Need help?" She looked up, and Lucas smiled at the guilty expression on her pretty face.

"Why is this locked?"

He shrugged and whipped out his keys, then opened the door. He pushed, and it swung wide. Angela stared like an idiot at the half-painted room. A white rail lined the wall, and there was a mural of meadows and fluffy white clouds near the ceiling painted all around the room. Below the rail was wallpaper that looked like a picket fence.

Her throat thickened as she stepped inside, onto the tarp. "You did this?"

"Had to have something to do for the past couple

of weeks." *Alone, without you. Missing you,* Lucas wanted to say but treaded carefully.

Angela moved closer to the walls. There were little sheep eating flowers, ducks in the pond, a little farmhouse in the distance. "This is incredible," she said.

"I haven't got the clouds just right, though." He crossed to the sponge and paint, opened the can, stirred a little before dipping, then reached high to press more white onto the blue of the sky.

"I knew you could draw, but I didn't know you were this talented."

"Me, neither. Who'd have figured that one, huh? I learned how to do this from watching one of those home improvement shows." He blotted once, twice, then stood back to survey his work.

"Do you really think a child will notice whether the clouds are perfect or not?" she asked.

"Nah, but I will."

"Why are you doing this all now, Lucas? It's a little soon, you know. Something could happen."

"Nothing is going to happen to our baby." He shot a glance over his shoulder, his look fierce. "Nothing."

"Do you think this will convince me you want to be a dad?"

"I *will* be a father, Angel. But do I still have to convince you?" He held his breath, still looking over his shoulder, his hand poised to apply more paint.

"No, you most definitely don't. Not anymore."

Smiling, he faced her, laying the cloud-shaped sponge aside and snatching up a cloth to wipe his hands. "Good, finally."

She took a step back.

His smile fell.

"I know you want the baby. You've never had any family except mine."

Lucas felt a chill crawl up his spine.

"And now I'm carrying your only real family."

"Ours," he growled.

"And just how am I supposed to take that? Part of me keeps screaming at me, go for it. The man you've loved forever wants to marry you. You're having his baby and look how he's proving he wants this child now. Wants to be a part of her life." She waved to the painted walls. "But now the baby is the problem."

"No." His features tightened. "You're letting it be."

She shook her head. "I'm carrying the one thing you've lacked your entire life. Family."

His features tightened with anger. "Dammit, Ange, you've been my family. Now it's just growing larger."

Her heart caved a little, and the longer she looked at him, the more it cracked and fell to pieces. He never mentioned loving her. Never once mentioned *them*.

"I want to marry you," he said. "I want our baby to have a better start than I did. And I want that start to begin with you and me, together. What else can I do?"

When she didn't answer and simply stared at him, Lucas saw her heart breaking right before his eyes and felt confused and helpless.

"Do?" She sighed. He was doing all the right things, just not saying them. A baby and supplies and a marriage license didn't make a family, she thought. Love did. She wasn't going to push him into committing to her if he couldn't admit his feelings to himself. She loved him, had shouted it to the rooftops, but Lucas, she realized, would never be completely hers because he couldn't speak the same words out loud. To her.

And she couldn't go on being the only one who could.

He was still living his life inside his fear, as if he *might* want the chance to run. Still on the edge, not completely inside.

She might have his heart, but he wasn't ready to let her hold it, protect it.

Angela turned and walked out. He didn't call her back, didn't follow, and her heart shattered over and over as she hurried to her car. She barely glanced at the big black SUV sitting in the driveway where the silver Jaguar once was.

Big guns, she thought. All firing blanks.

For the only sounds she wanted to hear were three simple words.

In the studio, Angela sat at her console, feet propped on the desk, her head bowed. She felt drained even though she'd slept half the evening and hadn't gone to her Wife Incorporated job for the past few days. She really couldn't take another talk with Lucas right now and idly wondered what little toy or piece of baby equipment he'd bought. Then she realized she'd have to get the same things for her place.

A little moan of despair escaped her. Separate lives, separate homes for their child. It was like a divorce without ever being married. Her chest tightened, and she cursed her heart for being so damned stubborn. Especially when she knew now he wanted to be a father and wanted her to be his wife. And she considered that since she hadn't spoken to him in a week, she just might have pushed him too far away.

What do you want, for heaven's sake? a voice in her head asked.

All of it.

She wanted the great guy with the great career, the back yard full of kids and the house with a white fence, and dammit, more than anything she wanted Lucas to love her. *Her.* Not because of a baby, not because she wanted to hear it, but because he *needed* to say it. Because he wasn't scared of committing the rest of his life to her without those words.

For with Lucas, once said, she knew it was true and forever.

He'd never uttered them before.

And she doubted he would now.

Her producer tapped the glass, and Angela flinched, then looked at the red light flashing the phone line. A caller. Wonderful, she thought, and punched the button.

"Hi, this is AJ, you're on the air."

The caller cleared his throat, then said, "Hi."

Angela rotated her hand, silently encouraging the caller to talk. "What can I help you with tonight?"

"Well, there is this woman."

"And? Is she making you miserable or deliriously happy?"

The caller chuckled. "A lot of both, as a matter of fact."

"Do you love her?"

"Oh, yes. For a very long time. I want to marry her."

"Does she love you?"

"Yes, I have no doubt about that."

She frowned at the microphone arching over her desk. "Then what's the problem?"

"She doesn't believe that I want to marry her for the right reasons."

"And those are?"

"Barring details, well...we've had a relationship for years. We've been friends. Recently we've taken it further."

Angela swallowed, her heart suddenly beating double time. "Go on."

"I've always wanted this, but never dared because she was the best thing that ever happened to me, and I didn't want to ruin it."

"And this further step...you think you've ruined it."

"No, it made us stronger."

"Why wouldn't she want to take it further?"

"I've had this problem with commitment, and she knows it. She's always known it. It's a little of what's kept us friends, and only friends, for so long."

A chill tightened Angela's spine just then, and she slid her feet off the desk. "Is it true?"

"It was, but now…"

There was a stretch of silence on the air. Angela felt her palms sweating. "Talk about it. That's what I'm here for."

"I've dated a lot of women who I've liked but *never* loved. Women who I knew deep down were not what I wanted in a wife. They were the complete opposite of her."

"Why do you think you did that?"

"Because I was protecting myself."

"From what?"

Someone tapped the glass of the studio, and Angela looked up as Lucas stepped before the window, holding his cell phone to his ear. She inhaled sharply, glancing at the computer screen, the mike, then back to him.

"From what, caller?" She managed to speak over the knot in her throat.

Lucas opened the door and stepped inside the booth. "From committing to anyone but her."

Her heart jumped in her chest. "Why?" Angela rose slowly as he moved around the desk.

Inches from her, he said, "Because she is the only person who has stuck by me, loved me for the man I am, not what I have. Or who I will be. She's the only one I *can* commit to. Because I've been hers since the day she asked me to walk her home from school."

Angela's eyes burned as she gazed at him. "Personally, I think she's been a fool."

"Ah, but she had good reason to doubt me." Luc shut off the cell phone.

Angela pulled off the headset and tossed it aside.

Her grinning producer opened the sound to the air-waves, and their words broadcasted across two states.

Neither noticed.

"Why is that?" Her voice shook with her emotions.

"Because I forgot that you were a woman first and my friend second. I forgot to tell you that when I see you, everything in me jumps to life, that to look in your eyes is like losing a breath, and knowing you love me is like coming home, like heaven. I didn't tell you that I don't just desire you. Desire is a whim. I *need* you...to be whole." He swallowed, his Adam's apple scraping his dry throat. "I need you because I'm missing half of me when you're not near, and when we're apart...ah, God," he said, gazing deep into her eyes. "I feel as if I can't survive till we're together." He leaned forward, brushing his mouth over hers, and felt her lips tremble, heard her soft telling whimper. "See, I forgot," he whispered. "I forgot that just because I've known you for so long, shared everything with you, that I hadn't really shared what was hiding in my heart."

Her gaze rapidly searched his. "What are you saying, Lucas?"

"I love you."

Her eyes immediately teared, her heart filing with sweet music.

He cupped her face in his palms. "I love you, Angel. And I can't love anyone else, I never could...because I've loved you for fifteen years, and there just isn't any room for another woman. There never has been."

"Lucas."

His eyes burned as he sank his fingers into her hair, his gaze locked with hers and his emotions pouring through each word. "I love you, baby. I want to be your husband, your lover, the only person you turn to, the one who'll keep your secrets and share your dreams." He brushed his mouth over hers, once, twice, then said, "I don't know how to prove that I love you and I want to marry you, and not just because of this b—"

She put two fingers over his lips. "You just did."

His smile was slow and bone-racking sexy as he kissed her fingers, turned his face into her palm, briefly closing his eyes. "Then say you'll marry me." He looked at her, this woman he loved, this woman he wanted more than air, and produced a beautiful diamond solitaire. Taking her hand, he poised it at her fingertip. "This is only the beginning. Angel, say yes."

Angela stared at the ring, her heart slipping up to her throat. "Yes," she whispered, and her gaze flashed to his. "Oh, yes."

Grinning, he pushed the ring onto her finger. Her hands slid up his chest and wrapped around his neck. Tears rolled down her cheeks unheeded, and he pressed his forehead to hers.

"I love you, medicine man," she said softly.

He grinned, wide and filled with happiness. "I love you, Angel."

Then suddenly, he grabbed her tighter, tipping his head back to let out a rebel yell as he lifted her off the floor and turned her in a quick circle.

She laughed tearfully, clinging to him, loving the feel of him in her arms again and never wanting to let go.

Then he crushed her mouth beneath his and crushed her body against his own, feeling her mold to him, fill the spaces like she filled the emptiness in his soul. Her fingers threaded through his hair, and he moaned over the simple pleasure of her touch and rejoiced at what the next sixty or seventy years would bring to him.

To a man who had nothing and now had it all.

A shaky voice peeled into the soundproof booth. ''Ah, Angela, Miss Justice. Help. The phone lines are all lit.''

Ignoring the voice, Lucas gazed down at her, brushing her hair from her face, absorbing her beauty, the love he could feel radiating from her and into him. He felt complete, home at last.

His life, he thought, would only get better.

''Miss Justice?'' her young producer squeaked.

''Take a message,'' she said, gazing into Luc's ice-blue eyes and knowing without a shred of doubt that the lonely, dangerous boy she'd met years ago was gone, his secret fears dissolving, and in her arms was a man ready to embrace the future, share a love they both knew would last their lifetime and beyond.

Epilogue

Ten years later

"**G**o, Lucas! Go!" Angela yelled as her husband took third base and raced for home plate.

"Gosh, Mom, could you be any louder?"

Angela looked at her oldest son, Nick, grinning. "Yup." She looked at home plate in time to see Lucas slide the last few yards and touch the base. She cheered, doing the happy dance for the man she loved.

And she hoped he hadn't broken something doing that.

Her son rolled his eyes and shrank in his seat. Angela laughed and bent to kiss the top of his head. "I hope all your friends are watching."

Nick groaned and looked at his grandfather. "Was she always like this?"

Evan grinned and rubbed the boy's shoulder, his granddaughter on his lap. "Yes, son, sorry."

Nick fought a smile.

"You know," Evan said, "your mom plays ball better than your dad."

"No way." The boy looked horrified.

She looked at her son. "Who do you think taught him?" she said, then winked.

Nick looked skeptical, then gave in. His mom wasn't exactly normal. There wasn't much she couldn't do or wouldn't try, and Nick smiled at that. He did have the best mom in town. "How come you never told?"

"A gal's got to have some secrets. Right, girls?"

Her daughters smiled at her, then Bridget made a prissy face at her older brother. Caroline copied her, as usual.

"Come on. Let's congratulate your dad," Angela said, making her way among the moving people. Angela flew down the steps and slammed into him.

He groaned at the impact.

"Hurting?" she said for his ears alone, then kissed him quickly.

"A little." He wrapped his arm around her waist and walked with her toward the stands. "Good grief, I'm too old for this." He pushed off his ball cap and ruffled his damp hair.

"I know something you'll never be too old for," she said with a sly look.

"Oh, yeah?"

"Yeah, you do look terribly sexy in that uniform."

He grinned and kissed her deeply, a little more slowly.

She eased back, breathless, then glanced at the stands. "Now buck up. Your son thinks you're a god and I'm nothing short of a loud embarrassing female."

Lucas frowned, then glanced at his son coming toward them. "Guess we need to have a little chat?"

"Nah, he'll get over it. It's a testosterone thing. He's half child, half teen and wants to be a man."

"Lord, I'm glad you're a psychologist."

She winked at him. "I do have my moments."

"More than moments, darlin'," Lucas said, and his hand slipped discreetly lower on her hip.

She nudged him. "Save that till after the hot shower and half a pound of Ben-Gay you're gonna be begging for later."

"I don't beg."

"Wanna bet?" she said, wiggling her eyebrows and reminding him of the last time they'd managed to get a few private moments alone.

Despite his exhaustion, the memory made him hard. "You're gonna beg this time."

"Talk, talk, talk," she said and backed out of the way as their children raced toward them.

Lucas's heart lifted as his son skipped to a stop, his sisters trailing at a dainty speed.

"Not bad, Dad," Nick said, taking his father's cap and glove. "Nice base hit."

"Thanks, son." Lucas closed his arm around his

boy's shoulder, smiling. "Your game's on Wednesday, right?"

Nick nodded.

"Then this weekend we'll have to practice your swing, what do you say?"

"Great!" The boy grinned, thoughts of hitting one out of the ballpark for his father running through his mind.

Lucas ruffled his hair and smiled, thinking about how much fun it was being a dad.

Then he let his wife and son go as his daughters scrambled to be the first to greet him. Scooping them up, he planted a sweaty kiss on their cheeks and laughed when they made faces and rubbed it off. He tried to look offended. But they just giggled, and he put them down.

Their three children scampered ahead to join their cousins. As he and Angela approached the stands, he let his gaze wander over the people making their way down the bleachers. And he realized the stands were filled with his family.

Only his family.

"What's so amusing?" Angela asked when she saw that odd smile.

"Nothing," he replied, greeting the clan with a wave. Yet he wondered when he'd stop marveling at that, stop getting this giddy feeling when he realized he wasn't alone and never would be again.

Almost like the feeling he had when he looked at his wife.

As if he were standing outside the high school, his hands shoved deep into the pockets of his jeans, trying hard to look invincible when his hair was covering his eyes and hiding the secret way he'd looked at her.

Like she was his the instant he wanted her to be.

And from that moment, Lucas knew he'd allowed himself the hope, the chance to know what it was to truly love and feel it in return. His teenage dreams had been fulfilled, and as he swung his wife into his arms, kissing her before the fading crowd, he understood all over again how lucky he was that day she'd said yes before two million listeners in two states.

The day he'd closed the door on his past and opened one to a wonderful, exciting future. With her.

And their kids.

And their aunts.

And uncles and cousins and grandparents...

* * * * *

THE
F RTUNES
OF TEXAS

invite you to meet

THE LOST HEIRS

**Silhouette Desire's scintillating
new miniseries, featuring the beloved**

FORTUNES OF TEXAS
and six of your favorite authors.

A Most Desirable M.D.—June 2001
by Anne Marie Winston (SD #1371)

The Pregnant Heiress—July 2001
by Eileen Wilks (SD #1378)

Baby of Fortune—August 2001
by Shirley Rogers (SD #1384)

Fortune's Secret Daughter—September 2001
by Barbara McCauley (SD #1390)

Her Boss's Baby—October 2001
by Cathleen Galitz (SD #1396)

Did You Say Twins?!—December 2001
by Maureen Child (SD #1408)

And be sure to watch for *Gifts of Fortune*,
Silhouette's exciting new single title,
on sale November 2001

*Don't miss these unforgettable romances…
available at your favorite retail outlet.*

Where love comes alive™

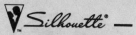

Silhouette®

where love comes alive—online...

eHARLEQUIN.com

your romantic escapes

—Indulgences—

♥ Monthly guides to indulging yourself, such as:
★ Tub Time: A guide for bathing beauties
★ Magic Massages: A treat for tired feet

—Horoscopes—

♥ Find your daily Passionscope, weekly Lovescopes and Erotiscopes

♥ Try our compatibility game

—Reel Love—

♥ Read all the latest romantic movie reviews

—Royal Romance—

♥ Get the latest scoop on your favorite royal romances

—Romantic Travel—

♥ For the most romantic destinations, hotels and travel activities

Feel like a star with Silhouette.

We will fly you and a guest to New York City for an exciting weekend stay at a glamorous 5-star hotel. Experience a refreshing day at one of New York's trendiest spas and have your photo taken by a professional. Plus, receive $1,000 U.S. spending money!

Flowers...long walks...dinner for two... how does Silhouette Books make romance come alive for you?

Send us a script, with 500 words or less, along with visuals (only drawings, magazine cutouts or photographs or combination thereof). Show us how Silhouette Makes Your Love Come Alive. Be creative and have fun. No purchase necessary. All entries must be clearly marked with your name, address and telephone number. All entries will become property of Silhouette and are not returnable. **Contest closes September 28, 2001.**

Please send your entry to: **Silhouette Makes You a Star!**

In U.S.A.	In Canada
P.O. Box 9069	P.O. Box 637
Buffalo, NY, 14269-9069	Fort Erie, ON, L2A 5X3

Look for contest details on the next page, by visiting www.eHarlequin.com or request a copy by sending a self-addressed envelope to the applicable address above. Contest open to Canadian and U.S. residents who are 18 or over. Void where prohibited.

Our lucky winner's photo will appear in a Silhouette ad. Join the fun!

SRMYAS1

HARLEQUIN "SILHOUETTE MAKES YOU A STAR!" CONTEST 1308
OFFICIAL RULES
NO PURCHASE NECESSARY TO ENTER

1. To enter, follow directions published in the offer to which you are responding. Contest begins June 1, 2001, and ends on September 28, 2001. Entries must be postmarked by September 28, 2001, and received by October 5, 2001. Enter by hand-printing (or typing) on an 8 ½" x 11" piece of paper your name, address (including zip code), contest number/name and attaching a script containing 500 words or less, along with drawings, photographs or magazine cutouts, or combinations thereof (i.e., collage) on no larger than 9" x 12" piece of paper, describing how the Silhouette books make romance come alive for you. Mail via first-class mail to: Harlequin "Silhouette Makes You a Star!" Contest 1308, (in the U.S.) P.O. Box 9069, Buffalo, NY 14269-9069, (in Canada) P.O. Box 637, Fort Erie, Ontario, Canada L2A 5X3. Limit one entry per person, household or organization.

2. Contests will be judged by a panel of members of the Harlequin editorial, marketing and public relations staff. Fifty percent of criteria will be judged against script and fifty percent will be judged against drawing, photographs and/or magazine cutouts. Judging criteria will be based on the following:

   - Sincerity—25%
   - Originality and Creativity—50%
   - Emotionally Compelling—25%

   In the event of a tie, duplicate prizes will be awarded. Decisions of the judges are final.

3. All entries become the property of Torstar Corp. and may be used for future promotional purposes. Entries will not be returned. No responsibility is assumed for lost, late, illegible, incomplete, inaccurate, nondelivered or misdirected mail.

4. Contest open only to residents of the U.S. (except Puerto Rico) and Canada who are 18 years of age or older, and is void wherever prohibited by law; all applicable laws and regulations apply. Any litigation within the Province of Quebec respecting the conduct or organization of a publicity contest may be submitted to the Régie des alcools, des courses et des jeux for a ruling. Any litigation respecting the awarding of a prize may be submitted to the Régie des alcools, des courses et des jeux only for the purpose of helping the parties reach a settlement. Employees and immediate family members of Torstar Corp. and D. L. Blair, Inc., their affiliates, subsidiaries and all other agencies, entities and persons connected with the use, marketing or conduct of this contest are not eligible to enter. Taxes on prizes are the sole responsibility of the winner. Acceptance of any prize offered constitutes permission to use winner's name, photograph or other likeness for the purposes of advertising, trade and promotion on behalf of Torstar Corp., its affiliates and subsidiaries without further compensation to the winner, unless prohibited by law.

5. Winner will be determined no later than November 30, 2001, and will be notified by mail. Winner will be required to sign and return an Affidavit of Eligibility/Release of Liability/Publicity Release form within 15 days after winner notification. Noncompliance within that time period may result in disqualification and an alternative winner may be selected. All travelers must execute a Release of Liability prior to ticketing and must possess required travel documents (e.g., passport, photo ID) where applicable. Trip must be booked by December 31, 2001, and completed within one year of notification. No substitution of prize permitted by winner. Torstar Corp. and D. L. Blair, Inc., their parents, affiliates and subsidiaries are not responsible for errors in printing of contest, entries and/or game pieces. In the event of printing or other errors that may result in unintended prize values or duplication of prizes, all affected game pieces or entries shall be null and void. **Purchase or acceptance of a product offer does not improve your chances of winning.**

6. Prizes: (1) Grand Prize—A 2-night/3-day trip for two (2) to New York City, including round-trip coach air transportation nearest winner's home and hotel accommodations (double occupancy) at The Plaza Hotel, a glamorous afternoon makeover at a trendy New York spa, $1,000 in U.S. spending money and an opportunity to have a professional photo taken and appear in a Silhouette advertisement (approximate retail value: $7,000). (10) Ten Runner-Up Prizes of gift packages (retail value $50 ea.). Prizes consist of only those items listed as part of the prize. Limit one prize per person. Prize is valued in U.S. currency.

7. For the name of the winner (available after December 31, 2001) send a self-addressed, stamped envelope to: Harlequin "Silhouette Makes You a Star!" Contest 1197 Winners, P.O. Box 4200 Blair, NE 68009-4200 or you may access the www.eHarlequin.com Web site through February 28, 2002.

Contest sponsored by Torstar Corp., P.O Box 9042, Buffalo, NY 14269-9042.

July 2001
COWBOY FANTASY
#1375 by Ann Major

August 2001
HARD TO FORGET
#1381 by Annette Broadrick

September 2001
THE MILLIONAIRE COMES HOME
#1387 by Mary Lynn Baxter

October 2001
THE TAMING OF JACKSON CADE
#1393 by BJ James
Men of Belle Terre

November 2001
ROCKY AND THE SENATOR'S
DAUGHTER
#1399 by Dixie Browning

December 2001
A COWBOY'S PROMISE
#1405 by Anne McAllister
Code of the West

MAN OF THE MONTH

For over ten years Silhouette Desire has been where love comes alive, with our passionate, provocative and powerful heroes. These ultimately, sexy irresistible men will tempt you to turn every page in the upcoming **MAN OF THE MONTH** love stories, written by your favorite authors.

Available at your favorite retail outlet.

Where love comes alive™

COMING NEXT MONTH

#1387 THE MILLIONAIRE COMES HOME—Mary Lynn Baxter
Man of the Month
Millionaire Denton Hardesty returned to his hometown only to find himself
face-to-face with Grace Simmons—the lover he'd never forgotten. Spending
time at Grace's bed-and-breakfast, Denton realized he wanted to rekindle the
romance he'd broken off years ago. Now all he had to do was convince Grace
that *this* time he intended to stay…*forever*.

#1388 COMANCHE VOW—Sheri WhiteFeather
In keeping with the old Comanche ways, Nick Bluestone promised to marry
his brother's widow, Elaina Myers-Bluestone, and help raise her daughter.
Love wasn't supposed to be part of the bargain, but Nick couldn't deny the
passion he found in Elaina's embrace. Could Nick risk his heart and claim
Elaina as his wife…*in every way*?

#1389 WHEN JAYNE MET ERIK—Elizabeth Bevarly
20 Amber Court
That's me, bride-on-demand Jayne Pembroke, about to get hitched to the
one and only drop-dead gorgeous Erik Randolph. The proposal was simple
enough—one year together and we'd both get what we wanted. But one taste
of those spine-tingling kisses and I was willing to bet things were going to get a
whole lot more complicated!

#1390 FORTUNE'S SECRET DAUGHTER—Barbara McCauley
Fortunes of Texas: The Lost Heirs
When store owner Holly Douglas rescued injured bush pilot Guy Blackwolf
after his plane crashed into a lake by her home, she found herself irresistibly
attracted to the charming rogue and his magnetic kisses. But would she be able
to entrust her heart to Guy once she learned the secret he had kept from her?

#1391 SLEEPING WITH THE SULTAN—Alexandra Sellers
Sons of the Desert: The Sultans
When powerful and attractive Sheikh Ashraf abducted actress Dana Morningstar
aboard his luxury yacht, he claimed that he was desperately in love with her and
wanted the chance to gain her love in return. Dana knew she shouldn't trust
Ashraf—but could she resist his passionate kisses and tender seduction?

#1392 THE BRIDAL ARRANGEMENT—Cindy Gerard
Lee Savage had promised to marry and take care of Ellie Shiloh in accordance
with her father's wishes. Lee soon became determined to show his innocent
young bride the world she had always been protected from. But he hadn't
counted on Ellie's strength and courage to show him a thing or two…about
matters of the heart.

SDCNM0801